S H A N E

A NOVEL BY

MARY A. WASOWSKI

Copyright © 2019 by Mary A. Wasowski
Cover Design by Francessca's PR & Design
Editing by Joe Marron
Formatting by JT Formatting

First Edition: April 2019
Library of Congress Cataloging-in-Publication Data

Wasowski, Mary A.
Shane / 1st ed
ISBN-13: 978-0-9969605-8-8

THE BRIGHTEST STARS IN THE SKY
ARE THE ONES THAT SHINE DOWN ON US.

PROLOGUE
Another time...another life

Shane

"I must be crazy for allowing you to talk me into doing this on the night before my wedding," I said to Jagger as I froze my ass off on the frozen lake. "What the hell are we doing out here?" I asked my crazy best friend.

"We are doing something that I didn't have a chance to do when I married Tenley last month, so I am passing on a Parrish family tradition down to you."

"And what might that be? We freeze our balls off? Yeah, Jag that will make for an interesting honeymoon with Shelby."

"Come on, Shane. Where's your sense of adventure? We used to do this all the time when we were younger. It was fun then, and it's fun now."

"It's not the same without Jamie. God! I miss him something fierce."

Jamie was Tenley's big brother and ours too. He was the best friend we would ever have in our lifetime. His life was cut short by cancer that had more power than modern medicine or all our faith combined, and now he was up in the stars watching over us.

1

"We all do, man, but he's here. Just raise your eyes up to the sky. His star is shining brightly down on us tonight."

"You really think so?"

"I know so. He was there in New York too when I married his sister. He's always with us Shane. You have to believe that, okay?"

"Okay."

I said nothing more on the subject, and although I froze, we did manage to catch some fish and talk for hours about all the great times we shared as friends. A conversation would not be complete without the mention of Jamie; he was our spirit animal in the sky. He always knew the right words to say to us when we needed to hear them, and if he ever doubted his own advice, he certainly didn't show it to us.

I shouted, "I'm getting married tomorrow, Jagger! Holy shit! I wasn't sure if I was ever going to see this day."

"Tell me about it. It's how I felt when I reunited with Tenley, and then to marry her in the same city she left me for all those years ago is just a mind-spinning, knock-you-on-your-ass epiphany life moment."

"Wow, that's one way to put it, but technically she went to Yale first, then came to New York."

"Gee, thanks, bud, for the correction."

"Just keeping it real. No problem, Jag."

"I'm sorry. I shouldn't have brought that up. We agreed a long time ago that the past is the past and that's where it shall remain."

"I know you're still in the newlywed phase, but you're happy, right?"

"Immensely. I feel nothing else. Tenley is the other half of my soul. I can't breathe without her. Having her away for five years was the hardest test of all the strength I possessed."

"Will I have that kind of love with Shelby? The kind you can't survive without?"

"Does your heart race when she's near?"

"Like a heart attack."

"Shane, you're ready, and she is too. You are going to have an amazing life with Shelby, and our kids are going to grow up together as best friends, and we will teach them everything about life, this ranch, and a lot of things the women in our lives would probably have us wait on, but yeah, she's the one. Let's get you home so you can get some sleep and marry the love of your life tomorrow."

"Thanks, Jag, and I mean for everything. Having you forgive me was something I never believed would happen, and now you're standing up for me tomorrow as my best man."

"Yeah well, I had some free time on my hands."

"Shane and Shelby have written their own vows to each other to unite them today in holy matrimony. The rings, please?"

Jagger handed me the rings that would soon be on Shelby's hand forever. I was so nervous, but when I looked at my beautiful bride, I calmed and looked over to the reverend to continue.

"Shane, please take Shelby's hand, and you can begin whenever you're ready."

"Thank you, sir."

I took Shelby's hand in mine and placed a kiss on her soft skin before reciting my vows. She looked stunning today in her strapless gown. I was weak in the knees when I saw her walking down the aisle toward me, passing our family and friends all smiling and crying as she got closer to the altar. I almost swept her up into my arms but held back. I knew if I kissed her, I'd be done. She squeezed my hand a little and brought me back to the reason we were here.

I whispered, "Sorry, babe, just lost in a good memory."

"I figured, but I thought I could help you along."

"Always looking out for me."

The entire church laughed, and then I smiled back at my bride, taking a deep breath as I began to recite my vows:

"You know me better than anyone else in this world, and somehow still you manage to love me. You are my best friend and one true love. There is still a part of me today that cannot believe that I'm the one who gets to marry you. I love you, Shelby, so very much. You are every part of me that's good, and these are my promises to you that I pledge forever and will always honor for the rest of my life.

I promise to encourage your compassion, because that is what makes you unique and wonderful.

I promise to nurture your dreams, because through them your soul shines.

I promise to help shoulder our challenges. For there is nothing we cannot face if we stand together.

I promise to be your partner in all things, not possessing you but working with you as a part of the whole.

Lastly, I promise you perfect love and perfect trust, for one lifetime with you could never be enough. This is my sacred vow to you, my equal in all things."

Jagger stepped up behind me and patted me on my back, congratulating me for getting through my vows without totally passing out. I'd been so nervous that I would forget a line, but I stayed up half the night memorizing everything I wanted to say.

I watched her hand off the bouquet to her maid of honor and then turn back to me, trying very hard not to cry.

"Wow! I didn't write as much as you did, and now I'm feeling kind of silly for what I did write, but I hope it conveys how much you mean to me and just how honored I am that I'm about to become your wife." I smiled and hit her with a wink to put her at ease.

She released a deep breath and unfolded the small piece of paper she had tucked inside of her bouquet.

"I take you to be my partner for life.

I promise above all else to live in truth with you and to communicate fully and fearlessly.

I give you my hand and my heart as a sanctuary of warmth and peace. I pledge my love, devotion, faith, and honor as I join my life to yours.

These are my promises to you. I love you, Shane."

I mouthed the words "I love you" and then said, "This is it, babe."

"Shelby and Shane, you have expressed your love to one another through the commitment and promises you have just made. It is with these in mind that I pronounce you husband and wife. You have kissed a thousand times, maybe more. But today the feeling is new. No longer simply partners and best friends, you have become husband and wife and can now seal the agreement with a kiss. Today, your kiss is a promise. You may kiss the bride."

The entire church erupted in applause as I took Shelby in my arms and kissed her beautiful plump lips which sealed us as one, forever as husband and wife. I'd never been happier.

"Shane!!! Omg! Get in here."

I practically dropped my coffee and darted up the stairs two at a time until I reached our bedroom, where my wife was jumping up and down in excitement.

"Baby, what's wrong?" I gasped, and that's when she handed me the white stick with two pink lines on it.

"You're pregnant? OMG! You have a baby in there?" I said and then dropped to my knees to place my hands on her flat stomach.

She giggled in her sweet voice, probably thinking I was being silly, but I didn't care. She made me so incredibly happy, and this news was the icing on the cake.

"I can't believe it, babe. Right now, there's a baby in your belly?" I whispered as I was getting choked up while stuttering over my words. I placed a kiss on her flat stomach where our baby would grow, and then I got up on my feet to kiss her.

"I am. We are. Are you happy?"

"Extremely. We're having a baby!" I shouted as loud as my voice allowed me to.

I threw my arms in the air and then swept my beautiful wife off her feet and made love to her for the rest of the day.

The past six months had been like a dream. We found out we were having a son, which I could not be more pleased about. Our son would grow up with Jamie Jr., Jagger and Tenley's boy, and I knew they would be best friends like Jagger and I were. I couldn't wait to teach him how to ride and do all the things that made my childhood awesome. Our fathers were our teachers, and there was not one thing we didn't know how to do on this ranch, and now we got to pass all of that knowledge to our sons.

Surrounded by pillows all around us, I held my beautiful wife in my arms. I loved these moments with her. She had her head on my chest, and I thought she might be asleep. Then she let out a soft sigh.

I asked, "Hey, what are you thinking about? You are too quiet. I'm not worried, because I know you're happy. You haven't stopped smiling since you told me you were pregnant."

"Happy is an understatement. I can't wait for him to be born. I love him so much already, and we still have a few months before he arrives."

"I know what you mean. It's amazing, isn't it?"

"It is. I just wish I was feeling a bit better."

I shifted a little so I could look at her. "You're okay, right? Have you been counting your kicks and tracking his movement on the baby chart?"

"Have you been reading the baby books again?" she asked while giving me a smirk.

"Yes, and you should be too. Shelby, are you okay?"

"Sure, I am. I guess it's new mom jitters."

"Dr. Tillman didn't mention any concerns at your last appointment, did he?"

"No, he said all was progressing along and I'm right on schedule. I guess I just would have felt more at ease if the baby was moving around more."

"Well, that's why I asked you about the kick count. Honey, if you want to give him a call and have another ultrasound performed, then I say let's do it. I don't want to see you worrying if a simple scan will make you feel better."

"It's fine, I'm just looking into things that are not there. I talked to my doctor about this, and he assured me at my appointment all was fine. You've had me pull back from working down in the stables and over at the dude ranch."

"Yes, and you know why. I asked you to take it easy and just work in the office, but you pushed yourself and almost got hurt."

"I was fine, Shane. You overreacted."

"Are we going to fight about this? Because if we are, you can forget it. When I saw Sampson nearly trample you, I thought my fucking heart had stopped. Knowing you are safe and at home gives me the peace I need to leave you each and every day while I go to work."

"Well, no worries there, because I'm home a lot." She went to move away from me, but I already anticipated this move and held her close to me.

"What about the nursery? You know my mom has offered to help you."

"I know she has, but I'm happier designing it myself."

"Fine. I was just pointing out that you are not as alone as you think you are."

"Shane, you've been working so much lately, you don't even stop home for lunch anymore."

"Babe, work never stops when you live on a ranch. I'm sorry I've been missing some time with you, but once I get home from my trip, I promise my schedule will lighten up a bit. You haven't said anything about it, but you know I have to leave at the end of the week, right?"

"Don't remind me," she said, begrudgingly.

"Shelby…" I whispered against her neck as I pulled her closer to my side, desperately wanting to end this bullshit between us.

"It's fine. I knew what I signed on for when I married you. This ranch is part of you, and I know you want it to be part of our son's life too."

"Shelby, you make it sound as if it's a prison sentence. Is that tone really necessary? It hurts my feelings. Are you not happy here? This is our home, a home that I built for us."

"Oh, Shane, I'm sorry. Call it pregnancy brain or whatever those stupid books say. I love you. I love our life here at Fairchild, and I know our son will too." She kissed me and then wrapped her arms around my neck, assuring me the best way she knew how.

My only problem was that once she touched me, I felt doubt, and I hated to ever feel that way. When I looked into her eyes, I wanted to see her happy eyes smiling back at me, but there was the doubt that made me not believe Shelby. I was better than this, and she was too. I shook it off and trusted that she would be as open and honest with me as I had always been with her.

"Okay, I'll be back in a week. I love you so much, and my parents, the staff, everyone is just a phone call away. Are you sure you don't want to stay up at the main house? Connie said she would love to have you."

"No, as kind as her invitation is, I would rather stay here in our house. Remember, I have a nursery to finish."

I sighed at Shelby's snarky response to my question. I tried a different approach. "Will you call Tenley? Maybe you can have lunch or go into town and do some shopping together."

"Shane, I appreciate what you are trying to do here, but I am fine. Go on your trip and hurry back so I can stop missing you."

"That's my girl. I love you."

"I love you too."

I grabbed my duffle and headed over to my truck, looking back just enough over my shoulder to notice Shelby wiping away her tears. *Fuck!* It was killing me to leave her like this, and I hated myself for not running back to the house and just saying the hell with my business, but I started the engine and kept on going.

Although I cut it short by a couple of days, my trip was successful. I couldn't wait until the horses I acquired for Fairchild to arrive. They were just gorgeous, and the guys were going to go nuts over them.

Unfortunately, I had minimal contact with my wife, which just hurt my heart. I got her voicemail a few times, and when we did talk, all she kept saying was that she and the baby were fine. Again, I doubted it, and that was when I decided to jump in my truck and make my way back home.

I was on the road when Shelby called me in hysterics to the point that I could not understand what she was saying. It took me a few tries to calm her.

"Shane, I think something's wrong. Where are you?" she cried through the phone. Just hearing the fear in her voice made the hairs on my neck stand up.

"Baby, I'm still hours away from the ranch. What's going on?"

"The last couple of days I haven't been feeling the baby as much, and I'm really scared. I should have gone in yesterday, but I thought I was just being paranoid."

"Listen to me, Shelby. I want you to take some calming breaths. I'm going to hang up with you and call for help, and then I will call you back. Do you understand?"

"Yes, okay. Please hurry."

After I dialed 911, I called Jagger, but my call went straight to voicemail, and then it was the same with Tenley. I was trying to stay focused on the road while deciding who I could call. Everyone I knew and trusted was not answering their phones. I took a breath of my own and then called back Shelby, who was in a complete panic and crying, which left me devastated.

"Shelby, listen to me. I want you to stay put and wait for the ambulance that I had dispatched to you. I've called Jagger and Tenley too. Once they call me back, I will have them go to you. Please, just stay there and wait for help to arrive. I am driving as fast as I can to reach you, but for now, you have to depend on our friends."

"No! I need you. Why Shane? Why did you leave me? And especially now when I need you—no, *we*—need you the most. This can't be happening. Our baby has to be alright."

"Shelby, calm down and breathe. I love you so much, and I love our child. I would have never left had I known you weren't feeling well. You are not due for two months, and I saw no risk of leaving for a few days."

"You never do, do you, Shane? You are so damn selfish and only care about this fucking ranch."

"Baby, that's not true. I love you. I love our life and our child. Please just calm yourself and breathe for me. I am on my way."

"I'm not waiting. I can get into town quicker than the ambulance can get to me. Just meet me there if you could find the time."

"No! I need you to stay where you are. The roads are snow-covered and treacherous if you're not careful. Hello? Shelby?"

The line went dead and so did my heart. *What the fuck!* This was not Shelby, and to say that bullshit to me was definitely not my sweet wife who showered me with love every second of every day. This was the fear talking.

I quickly called Jagger, and my call went directly to voicemail. *Fuck. This is not happening.* I was making another call to my mom when Jagger finally called me back.

"Jagger, thank god. Where are you, man?" I asked frantically.

"Shane, when you called me, I was way up past the north ridge of the ranch and only had my horse as my means of transportation. It took me some time to get back down to the stables, where I could get my truck. Once I heard your message, I got home as fast as I could. I'm in my truck now, making my way to your place."

"Where's Tenley? I called you both. Dammit, Jag, I thought you two were together when I called."

"Shane, it's a work day here on the ranch. In case you have forgotten, my wife doesn't run cattle and fix fences. Tenley is at home with Jamie, who is nursing a bad cold right now. I told you that the last time we spoke. She probably didn't hear her phone because she's too busy tending to our son. Listen, man, I'm almost there. Don't kill yourself getting here."

"I'm sorry, Jagger, but it may be too late. I just got off the phone with Shelby, and she's frantic. She refused to wait for the ambulance and took off on her own, but not before hanging up on me."

"Oh shit! Okay, I'm just pulling up. She drives the red Dodge, right?"

"Yeah, is it there?"

"No, only the ranch truck is here. Okay, she couldn't have gone far. Let me double back, and then as soon as I catch up to her, I will call you."

"Thanks, Jagger. Please hurry."

I disconnected my call with Jagger and just prayed. When I finally reached the Wyoming state line, the feeling of dread was unraveling me. I repeatedly phoned Shelby, filling her voice mailbox. I kept on driving until my best friend called me back. I tried not to focus on the time and listened to music to keep me from going completely insane. I was never a patient man, as the minutes felt like hours ticking by.

I passed the turn off that would bring me home to the Fairchild Ranch when my phone buzzed in my pocket. The familiar ringtone belonged to Jagger, and my heart just about sunk deep into my chest. Answering it on the second ring, I barely got out a simple hello before

Jagger started talking.

"Shane, you need to come to the hospital. It's bad, bro. Shane, are you there?" he asked.

"I'm on my way." I disconnected the call and floored it until I reached the town limits of Jackson Hole. I'd been driving what felt like endless hours. I finally reached the medical center and then hurried to the emergency room, not caring where I left my truck. As I made my way inside, all eyes were on me as Jagger slowly approached me.

"Where is she? Where's my wife?" I shouted.

Grabbing me by my shoulders, Jagger said, "Shane, thank god you are here."

"Just tell me, man." I tried to move past him, but he held me back.

"There's been an accident."

"Yes, I know. Now what the fuck happened?"

"Shelby and the ambulance somehow collided with each other, causing her vehicle to flip off the road. By the time I reached the scene, Shelby was unconscious and pinned beneath the steering column of her truck. The Jaws of Life chopper arrived after the EMT's dispatched them to her location. She was airlifted here and immediately taken into surgery."

I bit back the tears threatening to fall. I knew I had to be strong for Shelby and our child.

"Shane," my mother called out as she tried to take me in her arms. "Oh my god, you're here. We've been so worried."

I then noticed my father, Brock, and Ren all back from their trip with all eyes on me. My mom was still trying to get me to connect with her, but I was numb. My father walked up behind my mother and then held my face in his strong hands and leaned his forehead up against mine.

He said, "I see it in your eyes, and I feel it on your skin. You are seconds away to losing your shit, but hold on, son, for your wife and child. Hang on, you hear me?"

When my eyes met his concerned ones, I simply nodded in agreement. He then took me in his arms and gave me a bear hug. My mother led me over to the waiting room, where I took a seat. I felt as if I was going to collapse from exhaustion and my fear was getting the best of me, not knowing anything about my wife. My eyes were burning with unshed tears. The waiting was killing me.

I had been here for more than two hours with no word at all. I had just reached my limit of patience when I saw two doctors dressed in scrubs and Shelby's doctor, Dr. Tillman, walking beside them. They entered through the double doors and were walking straight for me. I stood immediately, with my parents on either side of me. Jagger was quietly waiting in the corner.

Dr. Tillman patted me on my shoulder, and then the other two men introduced themselves. "Mr. Rhodes, I'm Dr. Johnson, and this is my colleague, Dr. Kirkland. We operated on your wife."

"Please, just tell me. How is she?"

"With proper rehabilitation, your wife will make a full recovery. She has a few broken ribs, and her leg is fractured not broken. No visible swelling of the brain, just a laceration from hitting the windshield that has now been stitched up."

"And the baby? How's my son?" *no one answered.* I looked directly at Dr. Tillman, and asked my question again, but he looked crestfallen. He was more than a doctor to us, he was also a family friend who cared about us.

Dr. Johnson answered for him. "I'm sorry, Mr. Rhodes, but there was too much trauma to your wife's abdomen, and with the significant blood loss, she lost the baby. We had to perform an emergency hysterectomy to stop the bleeding. She had thrown a clot during surgery, and we were running out of time. I had no choice but to remove her uterus to save her life. I am so sorry, Mr. Rhodes."

"Shane, there's more," Dr. Tillman said.

"More?" I whispered. Dr. Tillman urged me to sit back down but I couldn't move my legs. I needed to hear it, all of it.

"Shane, in an emergency situation, more like a life or death situation, we have to act fast and do the best we can for our patient. In this case, we had two, and I knew I would do everything in my power to save your child, but what I didn't expect to see is that..." he hesitated and got choked up on his words. "Son, I knew right away the minute we made the incision. Your son's umbilical cord had a series of twisted knots that cut off his oxygen supply. After I examined him, his measurements and growth were on target to the pregnancy. This is rare, and no one could have known this was happening inside of her body. He must have died in utero, I'm estimating 24 to 36 hours ago. I can't stress this enough to you that no matter the circumstance, there was no preventing this from happening. She did everything right in her pregnancy, and I know you long enough to see the guilt already in your eyes. You did nothing wrong. It just happened, and I am so sorry for your loss."

"I am so sorry for your loss." The words kept playing on a loop in my head and would not stop. I looked around the crowded room to see every single person who loves us just cry and comfort the other, while I feared I would never feel anything again.

"Shane, do you want to see him?" he asked. I sat in silence remembering every single moment I felt my son kick from inside Shelby's stomach. It was amazing knowing our love created another life and now he's gone. No, I can't do it. I have to remember him how I pictured him in my mind. I couldn't form the words to say to Dr. Tillman, as I fought back the pain of our loss. I moved my head from side to side and that was all I could manage before I fell apart. I watched Dr. Tillman let out a breath and turn to walk out of the waiting room.

At that moment, I felt as if my world had completely shattered into millions of broken pieces, ones that would never be put back together again. My hands began to shake, and then the rest of my body succumbed to the severity of what I was just told. I slowly dropped to my knees and roared out my pain, pounding my fists on the hard floor. I felt my father and Jagger at my back, but I shoved them away while I continued to punish myself. My knuckles were torn open and my hands were covered in blood as the realization hit me right through my chest.

The dream of becoming a father had died alongside that country road all because I wasn't here for my wife and child.

Where do we go from here? And how am I supposed to tell her that our son was dead?

1

Still broken

Shane

Another day in the life of my daily hell. I kept replaying the argument over in my mind and the way I left. I just couldn't breathe. It felt as if I was choking, and if I didn't do something quick, then I would have completely suffocated on the words that she had shouted at me. This was no way to live and I didn't know what to do to help my wife or myself. All I knew was that we have never been the same since our son died.

"What are you doing, you stupid asshole?" I shouted out to myself into thin air.

I held my head in my hands in defeat. Here I was, alone and playing out every detail of the argument I had with my wife and how I walked out on her and blocked out her calling out, begging me to come back. I should have stayed, but I had reached my limit with the distance that had been between us for more than a year, and I was suffocating from it.

"Where are you going?" she shouted at my back as I was headed for the door.

"I'm leaving, Shelby. Isn't that what you want me to do? I can't

change the past. Lord knows I wish I could, but I can't. I love you and a part of me always will, but I can no longer live—no—exist in this life with you when all you feel when you look at me is contempt. He was my son too, and somewhere deep and buried in your grief, you have forgotten that."

She gasped and began to cry, but I said nothing more and didn't attempt to comfort her. I remember seeing something shift in her eyes after I mentioned our son, and then I couldn't stand there any longer while she cried. I left and prayed I could drown out the memory of her calls to come back.

I wasn't going to lie; I missed my wife. I loved my wife. Before my signal totally cut out from being far out into the mountains, I had dozens of missed calls from Shelby.

How many times could I allow her to shatter and break me down? I was barely hanging on, and this last fight may have been the worst one yet. Since the moment we lost our son, we've been here, but in our hearts, someplace else. I worked the ranch day in and day out, and Shelby fell deeper into depression. When she was lucid, she yelled and blamed me for not being there for her and for choosing the ranch over her and our child. Those times cut me like a knife. I've bled out more times than I care to ever revisit. I meant every word I said to my wife before I walked out. I wish I could turn back time to the night that had led me here wallowing in my own guilt and facing the reality that I cannot change what happened to our child and the life we once had together.

After the words crossed over the doctor's lips, it was hard to piece together what followed next because it was all a blur. I remember Jagger and my father trying to pull me up from the floor, but I punched and shoved at them until they finally stepped away and just allowed me to feel the enormity of the situation I was in. My hands were a bloody mess, and once I stopped fighting and just completely fell apart, that's when I allowed my family to help me. My mother was crying, and the look on her face when she had to witness me hurting myself was just one more memory I want to forget. Deep down I knew my place should have been with Shelby, but I also needed to let go of some of the rage I had felt, knowing my son was dead.

I had been up here for hours getting lost in my memories, the most painful ones of my life. Just me and my horse looking out to the Teton Mountains and hoping for a sign, anything that would give me clarity over what my life had become.

I continued to look out and just breathe in the cool mountain air. I knew once I was up here, I wasn't going anywhere. I pulled out a bottle of whiskey from Yankee's saddlebag and began to gulp down the brown liquid that burned my throat. *Shelby already hates me, so why not get drunk and just add one more reason to her long list of reasons to keep on hating me?*

Once the alcohol began to do its job and numb my feelings, I sat my ass down and rested up against the tree. My eyes found the night sky, and there he was—Jamie, my brother and best friend—shining down on me.

Jagger told me that on the night his son was born, he looked up to the sky and found the brightest star he could find. He knew then it was Jamie, our brother and friend. He would forever be our guiding light from the heavens above to help us find our way when we needed him most. *Is this one of those times?* I needed him more than ever and prayed he would help me. He was the philosophical one from our group, but hell, he sure made a lot of sense.

As I continued to drink, I hoped I would just pass out, but my pain was too great for that. It had been hours since I left on Yankee to clear the ravaging thoughts that occupied my mind. It was the only way I knew how, to just ride and fly as fast as my horse could take me in the hopes that I would be able to breathe life back into my lungs and feel something for a goddamn second and remember what it meant to be alive. Because after the worst year of my life, I still feel...*dead.*

My eyes began to close when I heard a familiar voice.

"You know, if you were planning to stay up here all night and drink yourself to death, maybe you should have brought your pack with you. At least you would be warm once the buzz of that cheap whiskey wore off."

I looked up and saw my father standing before me.

"What are you doing here?" I asked with defensiveness in my tone.

Seeing my father here felt as if he was crossing some arbitrary line and crowding me when all I wanted was to be alone.

"I could ask you the same thing, Shane. What are *you* doing? How much deeper are you going to sink into your black hole? Drinking and riding is never a good combination."

Black hole? Yeah, that's a good word to describe where I am emotionally. I was angry and didn't care how much of an asshole I appeared to be to my father. I just wanted to lash out, and since he was here, and uninvited, it might as well be towards him.

"Gee, I don't know, pop. Maybe I'll just stay right here and finish off this whiskey and freeze to death. It's not like I'll be missed anyway."

"Get up!" he shouted.

"No!" I replied in defiance.

"Shane, get the fuck up and stand on your feet like the man I raised. I will not ask again."

"No!" I shouted louder toward my father, but not before I said, "Fuck off, and leave me alone."

Once the words passed over my lips and registered with my father, it didn't take long for the bear of a man my father was to pull me up by my shoulders and shove me into the tree I was leaning against. Then a right hook to my jaw landed me back on the hard ground.

"Leave you alone? Hell no! For what? So you could lose yourself in your pain and forever separate yourself from the ones who love you? Hell will freeze over before I allow that to happen." He knelt down where he was now eye to eye with me. "I won't pretend to know how you feel and what you've been through, but son, running away and hiding up here all day and every day will not bring him back. All it is proving is that you are further slipping away from Shelby and your family. We need you, son. Please, come home."

"She blames me, daddy. It's my fault."

"No, son, it's not. It was an accident. A horrible, unforgiving accident. It's not your fault. How many times do I have to say these words for you to believe them? As for Shelby, she's so lost in her own grief that she can't see how much she's hurt you along the way. Shane, you can't give up and hide up here drinking and talking to the clouds. You need to go back."

"For what? So my wife can tell me she hates me again? Don't you get it? I should have been with her. If I was, then she would have never been driving on that road, and we would be holding our child today."

"Shane, stop it. Blaming yourself will not bring him back. It's only going to destroy you in the end. I know you don't want to hear this, but you need to. Why was Shelby on that road to begin with? Hmmm? Tell me, son."

"She felt something was wrong and wanted to get to the hospital."

"Exactly, and knowing help was on the way, she didn't wait and still went on her own."

"Don't blame her. Don't you dare." I lunged toward my father to strike back, but he was quicker and grabbed my fist with his one hand.

"Stop it, Shane. Don't you do something you cannot take back. You must listen to me. I am not blaming Shelby, but you have to look at the full picture here. Shelby is part of this just as much as you are. You were not a neglectful husband that just took off and left his pregnant wife home alone. She had a few months to go in her pregnancy, and for all you both knew, everything was going well with no complications. Look at the ranch we live on; she could have called any number of ranch hands to help her. Yes, I know some of us were away, but she was never alone. She made a conscious choice to leave and not wait for the help that was coming. I'm so sorry, son, but all of this guilt you are carrying around just can't be on you."

"No, you're wrong. I shouldn't have left her."

"And, she shouldn't have been driving. Son, despite all the facts that led up to the accident and the grave loss that followed, you still need to keep in mind the reason behind Shelby wanting to get to the hospital in the first place. Something was wrong with the pregnancy, and it was fear that drove Shelby to do what she did. It was her natural instinct as a mother to protect her unborn child. Accident or no accident, the result would have still been the same. He was stillborn, Shane. You heard what her doctors told you. She did everything right in the pregnancy. Every single day, she cared for herself and the child she was carrying, and there is nothing that she or you could have done to prevent what happened to your son. As much as it pains me to say this, it was just bad luck. The accident did not kill your son. Please, Shane, you need to believe that."

"Why are you doing this to me? I never thought you would be so cruel." I buried my face in my hands and cried.

"Look at me," he said. When I didn't respond, he shouted as loud as he could, "You must listen and really hear me, Shane."

He grabbed me by my shoulders to force me to look at him and worse—to hear what he was desperately trying to make me believe. "I am not saying this to hurt you. You need to see what is right in front of you. The autopsy results proved that he had multiple knots in his umbilical cord cutting off his oxygen supply. You know this, son. Dr. Tillman told you all of this so many times. He didn't suffer. He just fell asleep. By the time the surgeons got in there, he was stillborn. What followed next was a cruel twist of fate, not my words here today, son. You need to get a handle on your life before you completely spiral out of control and we lose you too."

He let out ragged breaths in defeat as I remained in his grasp, silent to his words. He threw his hands up in the air and cursed loud enough to scare the horses. "Dammit, Shane! It wasn't your fault!"

I dropped my head, and he knew I was gone. After the mention of our son, I had completely zoned him out.

"I love you, son. As much as you believe that you are alone, you're not. We will be waiting for you when you're ready." He mounted his horse and left me there alone to drown in my sorrow and pain, but most of all, my guilt.

2

Breaking point

Shelby

As much as I screamed for him to come back, deep down in my heart, I knew he might not be returning home. It was my fault, all of it, but something always kept me from making things right between us. He tried every day since the day we lost our son to make things right again for us, but all I had done since then was shut him out.

I'd been so cruel to Shane. How could I blame him for walking out on me? He did exactly what I wanted him to do. He left. I watched him walk away from me and our home and just leave. As I stood there on our porch screaming at him to get out, the realization hit me like a bullet to the chest that he might just listen for once and not come home to me. I immediately regretted my actions, but it was too late. He was gone. Shane was right. I never cared about his grief. I carried our son inside of me for all of those months, so naturally I believed I would be the only one to truly suffer and feel his loss. *Oh god, that's not true.* Shane wanted our son from the moment I told him I was pregnant. He loved him so much and was already an amazing father. *What have I done to us? And how do I get him back?* The fear that coursed through

23

me was crippling. What if he finally threw in the towel and closed the door to our marriage?

What was I doing? How could Shane stand to look at me after all I had done to him and to our relationship? By the time my brain connected with my heart, it was too late to reach him. I tried calling him back, but why would he answer when I begged him to go? I called and called him, but all my calls went straight to voicemail. I would be the last person he would ever want to speak with.

After a few hours passed, I just stood there in my big empty home, contemplating what I would do next. The gun cabinet that was off to the corner never looked more inviting. I could have my pick, and one single shot would end my misery, and Shane's too, for that matter. He would find me, feel hurt for a while, and then pick up the pieces of the wreckage that I would have left for him to clean up.

"What are you doing?" I said to myself aloud, and then I heard a familiar voice from behind me.

"Exactly. What in the hell are you doing, Shelby?"

I quickly turned around to see Wendy Manning here in my house.

"Well? Are you going to answer me, girl? Or are you going to stand there and stare at me like I just stepped on your grave?"

"Wendy, what are you doing here? How did you even get in?"

"The door was open, and I did knock a few times before letting myself in. Now, answer the question. What are you doing? And don't even try to lie to me. You're staring over at that gun cabinet like it's your last meal or something. Believe me, Shelby, that's not the answer you are looking for."

"Why? Does anyone really care if I am here or not? It would make Shane's life a hell of a lot easier."

"You selfish girl. You are so wrong. Hurting yourself would not only hurt Shane but complete the circle of hell he has been trapped in for the past year. You would finish him, and we would never get him back after that. He's up on the highest peak of this ranch right now, drinking himself half to death because of the guilt that is inside of him.

You never allow him to forget, do you, Shelby? I can't begin to know or understand you nor understand the loss you have had to endure, but I sure do recognize what pain looks like, and it's an emotion that Shane wears daily."

"Don't you see how much he loves you? How much he needs you to be healthy and whole again? You lost a child, not on your own, but together, you lost a child. It is an immeasurable amount of pain, but blaming Shane will not bring your son back. It's only going to drive him further away. You are so angry and blinded by the decisions you made on that day that you don't want to see or feel anything else. Please, Shelby, open your eyes and see the truth before it's too late. You are drowning just as much as Shane is, but allowing him to accept all the blame in this tragedy is not fair. The only person that could ever explain the reasons why your son is gone is God himself, and taking your life here today is not going to bring you any closer to him, nor the answers you desperately want. You will only drown deeper in your despair."

It was at that moment, my first moment of clarity, that I allowed myself to let go of all the pain and suffering I have felt since the day of my accident. I knew I was hurting over the loss of my baby, but not enough to hurt myself. I would never do that. I quickly got up from the floor and turned to look at Wendy, who had her arms open to me. I broke down into her arms as she held me as tightly as she could.

Wendy was like a second mom to everyone around here. She was the voice of reason and a constant support for Shane. I was the outsider of the group, but that was my fault. I never knew what it was like to be part of a close-knit family nor have close friends, for that matter. I didn't just marry Shane, I married the entire Rhodes, Fairchild, and Parrish families. They all accepted me with open arms and never once made me feel unwanted or unloved. And this was how I repaid that generosity...by hurting Shane, and worse, myself?

"There now, cry it out once and for all." She held me for the longest time until I finally stopped crying and wiped away my tears. I knew there would be more once I talked with Shane, but for now, I was okay.

"I'm so sorry, Wendy. How could you comfort me when I have been so cruel?"

"Easy, because I love you like a daughter. And Shane is the closest I have to a son, so there you go. Listen, Shelby, it doesn't have to be figured out all in one day. Lord knows you two have a lot of talking to do. Let us work on getting Shane home, and then it will be up to you on what comes next."

"Maybe I should go to him."

"No, you stay here. His father is up there now, and I would bet everything I have that it's not a pretty sight."

"I guess Mr. Rhodes can thank me for that. I hurt him, Wendy. It was awful."

"Now, stop it. Kip and Kathleen love you, and so does Shane. Whatever happens on that ridge is between father and son. What happens here in this house once Shane is home is between a husband and wife. You need to get yourself ready for that conversation. It's time, Shelby. It's time to let your husband back into your life and your heart."

"Does he want that, Wendy?"

"You are going to have to ask him. Prepare yourself for whatever his answer may be. He's been through a lot; you both have. What comes next will either begin the process of healing or break you forever. I will be praying for the better outcome."

"Thank you, Wendy, for everything. You have been the greatest friend. Shane is lucky to have you."

"I love you both, please know that. Shelby, when you met Shane, he was at a low point in his life. He had just lost his two best friends who were more like brothers: one for all eternity, and the other after a long list of circumstances. Dark times fell on Shane, and we were all very worried about him until he met you. You loved him enough for the both of you when he questioned how he felt. You didn't allow him to run away. You stayed by his side and showed him what you two could be to each other. When he married you on St. Valentine's Day, we had never seen him happier. He loves you, Shelby, and he will honor every single one of his married promises he made to you on that day if you just allow him to. All I ask of you is that if in your heart you don't feel you can find the love for Shane again, then please let him go. He's a good man and deserves good in his life."

"I still love him. I never stopped. I was just lost for a while." I could barely get the words out as they got caught in my throat. I have to make things right with my husband.

"Well, that's a start. Walk me out?"

"Of course, I will."

We walked side by side with her arm around my shoulders. We stepped off the porch, and then I hugged her again, needing and wanting her support. I knew I had it, but it was good to make sure. She returned my hug, smiled, and then got a strange look on her face. Wendy pulled away and looked up at the night sky as she leaned up against her truck.

"Wendy?" I asked. "What are you doing?"

"Hold on, darling. Give me a minute to find it. Yes, there he is."

"What is?" I was more confused than ever. She took my hand and directed it to the sky, finding exactly what she wanted me to see.

"There. Tell me what you see?"

Rolling my eyes, I said, "Stars, lots of stars."

"Yes, I see that too, but do you see one that stands out from the others?"

I looked all around and then found what she wanted me to see.

"Yes, that one," I said. "If I had to guess, it's right on the north ridge. I have never seen a star shine so brightly before."

"That's because that one is special, and only a precious few can see it when they really need to. You pray on it, and I'll make you a promise."

"I love your faith, Wendy, but I think I am going to need a lot more promises than just one."

"Trust me. You pray on that star. He'll hear you."

"Who will hear me? Wendy, I'm so confused."

"Just pray on it, and you'll get your answers. He's never let me down and will always be our angel in the sky."

I nodded and didn't question our wise friend. With one last hug, she climbed up into her big truck and sped off, leaving me alone with my thoughts and the bright star in the sky.

I put my hands together and closed my eyes before finding the star above. I prayed for Shane and hoped he would find his way home. I prayed for our son in heaven and hoped he was okay. But most of all, I prayed for forgiveness. I prayed for the chance to make things right with my husband. He deserved so much more than I'd been able to give him this past year.

I knew I made so many mistakes. Loving Shane Rhodes was not one of them.

I prayed I wasn't too late.

3

Crossroads

Shane

O nce I sobered up, I made my way down the mountain and back home to Shelby. It was late, and dawn would be greeting a new day in a matter of hours. After I settled my horse back into the stables, I contemplated on what to do next.

Do I just go inside and pack a bag? Or do I once again try to talk to my wife and beg her to listen to me? Our last argument did not end well, leading me to leave her crying and watching me walk away from the porch. Like always, her hurtful words were aimed directly at my heart. I kicked at Yankee to go faster to drown out Shelby's cries. How much more could I take?

My father was right. The longer I stayed up on that ridge and lost myself to my past, the further away I would be from my family. I knew I was loved and protected. I never doubted that ever, but when you lose something so great, a piece of you just dies along with it.

I was not immune to loss, not any one of us who lived on this ranch was. Losing Jamie, a friend who I loved as a brother, taught me that. What would he say if he were here today? I'm sure he probably would have kicked my ass by now and say just about anything to bring me back from the edge I was standing on. Jagger had tried—hell, everyone had—but I had refused them all. It took my father punching me yesterday to get me to come back home. *Now that I'm here, though, what the fuck do I do next?*

"Shane, is that you?" I heard her call out as she slowly came down the stairs.

I hadn't moved from my spot. I was just staring at my home and contemplating on what to do next. It was still dark outside with only the glow from the moon and stars above serving as our light.

"Yeah, baby, it's me. Go back inside before you get sick. It's cold out here." I said so easily as if this was just any normal work day on the ranch. She would always be waiting for me with smiles and hugs as I parked my truck and took her in my arms, kissing her until we were out of breath. *I miss those times.*

"Not until you do the same."

What? That was a far cry from the last time I was this close to Shelby. She actually sounded as if she cared.

I fisted my hands at my sides and looked up at her. Her eyes were glazed over with tears, and for the first time in a long while, she actually looked like my wife. The one who loved me once. The one who took vows with me and promised to love me forever. The one who promised me a house full of children, all before it was shattered by that damn accident.

"You go inside, Shelby, and I'll be right behind you. I need a shower first."

"Okay. You have to be hungry. Can I make you something?"

"Yeah, that would be fine." I swallowed hard, not knowing what else to say. *This whole interaction with Shelby was weird. What had happened to make her suddenly go sweet on me?*

I knew I smelled awful with the stink of cheap booze attached to my skin. I quickly made my way upstairs to shower and drown myself in the hot sprays of water. All the while in there, my head was spinning with what Shelby would say to me. I tried not to allow my mind to go to the worst-case scenario, but it was easy to do considering how we had been to one another this past year. No point in denying it, we'd been barely hanging onto each other.

Before making my way downstairs, I messaged Luke and Wade, my two top hands who worked for me here on the ranch. It would be time to begin the day soon with the morning chores and then all the daily tasks that followed. I was in no shape to work today in my hungover state, so I told them to manage without me and check-in with my father if anything would arise. I couldn't call my father yet, I wasn't ready for that conversation. The one with my wife would be more than I could handle. The guys would tell him that I was home, and at least he would know that I was safe.

Once I made my way down to the kitchen, Shelby was quietly waiting for me at the table. She had prepared breakfast for me, my favorite: steak and eggs. I grabbed a bottle of water and swallowed two Advil tablets to help with my headache, and I braced myself for what she would say.

To outside eyes, this scene would look totally normal: a wife preparing her husband's breakfast, with him thanking her appreciatively. My stomach rolled just at the normalcy of it, and eating was the last thing I wanted to do. I hadn't puked since my college days when I was young and stupid and didn't know any better.

I downed another water and finally took a seat at the table with Shelby's beautiful soul-sucking blue eyes on me, drawing me in and locking me in place. I could never resist her when her eyes met mine. They ignited something so deep inside of me that I had no control once I was caught and all that followed was me making love to her until we both reached the highs we needed to be fulfilled.

There was a time when I believed I would never get enough of Shelby, a time when she loved me with everything she had in her, but that was before. From where we were now, I didn't even recognize the couple we used to be, and it gutted me to know we may never get back who we were.

"Shane, please eat before it gets cold."

My stomach rolled again. Her voice was so soft and barely above a whisper, but laced with kindness. Hesitantly, I picked up my fork and took a bite of my eggs and then cut a few slices of steak. It was perfect, just the way I liked it. Her eyes looked hopeful as I continued to eat. It didn't take me long to clear my plate, making Shelby smile.

"Do you want anything else?" she asked.

I pushed my plate away and took in a few calming breaths before answering her. *Yeah, I want more, but it's not food,* I thought. My head was spinning with the after effects of all the alcohol I ingested yesterday, but more so from this scene right here in our kitchen.

"Shane? Are you okay?"

"What is this?" I asked.

"I don't know what you mean."

I slammed my hands down on the table, causing the dishes to nearly skip off the table. "This!" I stood and gestured to Shelby. "What the hell are you playing at? You hate me, remember? Aren't those the words you were shouting at my back as I walked out the door? You have me fucking spinning out of control, woman! Why are you doing this to me?"

I turned away from her and just wanted to run, but she stopped me by calling out for me to stay.

"I love you, Shane, and I am so sorry for hurting you. It wasn't your fault. It was no one's fault, just a very sad ending to a beautiful dream we both wanted."

I couldn't breathe. I felt as if my heart was going to beat out from my chest. *Does she love me? Is she sorry?*

I was white knuckling the countertop. I didn't know what to say or how to even respond to Shelby's truth, if that's what it was. I now felt her presence behind me as she put her hands on my hips. I tried not to jerk away, but it had been a long time for even the smallest of gestures. Once I calmed my breathing, she then moved her hands from my hips and wrapped her arms around my waist, with her face pressed against the middle of my back, breathing me in.

"Shane, please look at me. I need you." Her pleas just about broke me.

Turn around asshole, and talk to your wife. I was battling my need for self-preservation and trying to protect what was left of my heart. I let out a breath and finally turned to see the tears falling down Shelby's face, and I instinctively wiped them away.

"Please, baby, don't cry," I whispered as I cupped her face and leaned in to gently kiss each tear away. It felt like the most natural thing in the world to do. *How many times have I prayed for this moment where Shelby would come back to me?* Here she was in my arms, and for the first time in months, allowing me to touch her, kiss her, and love her. I didn't want to push my luck by wanting more, so I pulled back to look into her eyes and waited for Shelby to make the next move.

"Shane, do you still love me?"

I pulled back even further, questioning why she was asking me this.

She said, "I have made so many mistakes this past year, and I am truly sorry for every single one of them. You have every right to be angry with me. I know I've hurt you and broken you probably beyond repair, but before you walk out that door forever, will you please allow me to talk to you first? If, after everything I say, you still want to leave, then I promise I will not stop you. The last thing I want to do is bring you more pain. You never deserved it, and I blamed you for all of it."

Standing here and listening to my wife begging me to hear her felt mind-numbing. I couldn't find my voice to answer her, just allowed my mind to replay the last horrific year of our lives. It was moving in a fast-forward motion from the moment I knelt in front of her and kissed her swollen belly that day on the porch when I left for my trip, and then yesterday, where my father was screaming at me to come back. To be the son he raised. To be the man who vowed to love Shelby forever the day we committed our lives together.

I felt sick reliving the best and worst moments of our past. I wanted it to stop. I couldn't do this with her, not again. My stomach rolled, and I knew I couldn't hold back any longer. I rushed past Shelby and ran to the nearest bathroom. I emptied all the booze and the breakfast I had just eaten, with my stomach heaving and heaving until I had nothing left to expel. Shelby was right behind me rubbing my back and then cooling my neck with a washcloth.

I was still hugging the toilet when I finally asked her, "Why are you doing this to me? Why now, after all this time? I just don't understand you. You let me kiss you, dammit! You gave me hope in that kiss. It made me want more when I know I'm never going to have what I want. Why, Shelby?"

I cried like a fucking pussy and succumbed to the pain this heart and body was used to. I moved away from her and towards the sink to splash cold water on my face and clean my mouth but not before catching my exhausted reflection in the mirror. I was tired, so tired, and all I could do was lean against the wall and sink back to the floor in my despair. I looked up to my wife and said, "After all we have been through, how can you so easily tell me now that you love me?"

"Because I do love you. I never stopped loving you Shane, but for a long time what I felt for you was replaced with sadness and pain. I lost a child. Our child. And knowing that I can never have anymore was wrenching on my mind and spirit. I wanted to die, Shane, just die and join our son. I know I blamed you. I know how much I have hurt you with my words and actions. You leaving yesterday felt like my rock bottom. The thought of you never returning home to me scared me to death, and then being slapped back into reality from Wendy put everything into perspective for me."

"Wendy hit you?" I asked.

"No, not physically, but in a way she did. What she said to me after she found me in a heap of tears finally made me realize that if I didn't stop this continuous cycle of pain, I'm going to lose you—and us—forever. I have to tell you something else before you hear it from

Wendy."

"Okay, go on."

"I didn't hear her come in, and I have no idea how long she was standing behind me, but I was at a low point, probably the lowest, and I..."

"What? Tell me!" I demanded.

"I was staring at the gun cabinet and asking myself what I was doing. I swear, Shane, it was only for a second—less than a second—and then that's where the virtual slap comes in. She set me straight, and I'm so thankful to her. I see now how much she really does love all of you and would do anything for us. I swear to you, Shane, I wasn't going to do anything to harm myself. I was just alone and worried that our marriage was over and you had enough of me."

After hearing her words, I literally sprang up from the bathroom floor and took her in my arms, where she began to cry. It broke me so much every single time she cried, and although it killed me to see it, I knew I had to comfort her at the same time. I took her face in my hands and placed my forehead on hers, kissing her tears away as I made my way to her lips.

"You need to listen to me, and fucking hear me. Don't you ever entertain an idea like that again! No matter what happens between us, I can't imagine living in a world without you in it. No problem is too great that hurting yourself is the answer. Do you hear me?"

Trembling in my arms, she told me, yes, and then I kissed her again, with my wife giving me the access I needed. Even if this was our last moment to share, I knew I couldn't walk away from her without listening to all she wanted to say to me. The thought of that happening just about shattered whatever I had left of my heart, but I wouldn't walk out, not again.

When I pulled back, I just stared at her, easily getting lost in her blue eyes. She never could hide anything from me, especially when we were this close.

Shelby's eyes always held so much truth behind them. At this moment, I knew I had to give her a chance to explain her feelings. She reached for my hand, and I took it with no hesitation. I took a deep breath and prepared myself for what she would say next. *Would she heal us? Or break us forever?*

"I'm so sorry, Shane. I know I have been horrible to you, only caring about my feelings for a loss that was not just mine alone to bear but yours as well."

"Shelby, that's not true."

"Oh, Shane, there you go again defending my actions when we both know what I am saying is the truth. You said it yourself that I had forgotten about you and your grief, never giving you the same consideration you gave to me. I know I didn't have the sole rights to our son. He was yours too. You are such a good man, a better man than I probably deserve, but I know that I love you. If you could find it in your heart to give me another chance, I know I can prove to you that I was worth it—no, *we*—were worth taking a chance on. Please, Shane, will you give us another chance? A new beginning?"

Damn! She looked so beautiful with glazed over tears in her eyes. Once upon a time I saw dreams dancing in the beauty of her irises and it was lost to me for so long, and now I saw a glimpse of the woman I so desperately wanted to reconnect with.

Can I believe her this time? Can I really trust that she wants a reconciliation between us? My chest felt heavy with the many questions of uncertainty. I wanted to believe her so badly, and then I thought of all the wise people in my life screaming in my ear and telling me not to give up on my marriage.

She sat with her hands down on her lap and her eyes cast down in almost a submissive pose. She was giving me the lead to guide her in the direction I would choose for us. The ball was in my court. I lifted her chin with my finger and leaned in to place a soft kiss on her lips. A tear escaped and coasted down her lovely face. Even when she cried, Shelby was still so beautiful.

"I love you, Shelby. I never stopped, but you hurt me in more ways than I can explain, at least right now. I appreciate you telling me this, but I'm really tired and I just can't risk saying anything more to you that may come out the wrong way. I need to clear my head and think for a while."

"Isn't that what you did up on the ridge?"

"No. I was drinking my pain away. You should know, you put it there."

She stifled a gasp, and then I immediately felt regret in using my pain to hurt her back. She never lied or shied away from her feelings toward me. If anything, Shelby was honest and direct, whereas I was the one that was always tripping over my words. When she said nothing in return, I reached for her small frame and pulled her close to me.

"I'm sorry. I didn't mean that. This is why I need time. Don't you see? If I stay here with you, I am only going to hurt you, and that is the last thing I wish to do."

"Please, Shane, I can take it. Just don't go. If you don't want to talk, we don't have to. I just need to know that you are near, and I promise not to pressure you."

"Shelby, if what you said is true, then let me go and work it out. I will not leave the ranch, this I can promise, but this is all that I am capable of right now, okay?"

"Okay, I understand."

Something told me that she didn't, but she put on a brave face for my benefit.

I placed a kiss on the top of her head and then turned away from her. She didn't cry anymore. I suspect she would break in private, but as I stood in the doorway of the home I had built for us, all it felt like was just a shell of a broken foundation. I wanted nothing more than to take her in my arms and tell her everything was going to be okay, but how could I do that when I didn't believe it myself?

"I'm sorry, baby." I whispered. My back was to her as I faced the door. If I looked at her right now, I would surely break.

"I know you are, Shane. I'm not giving up. I'll be here waiting."

I said nothing more and walked out this time with only the sound of the door closing behind me. I turned over my truck, and the roar of the engine came to life. I didn't look back and drove on to where I needed to be. I prayed I would find what I was looking for because if I didn't, then I feared I would never get back to the man I was before hell rained down on me.

4

Forgiveness

Shane

O nce the house was no longer in sight, all I noticed was the rising sun in the background. The rays of sunshine served as a
beacon to where I needed to be. Once I was there, I felt his
presence nearly knock me over. I parked my truck by the river and
walked over to our spot. I guess you could say we all had our favorites
on the ranch, but this one in particular was definitely the best.

I shared so many memories here with Jamie and Jagger. After a
long, hot day working in the blazing sun, the three of us would come
down here and take a swim in the river. Most times it was brutally cold
from the mountains that surrounded it, but we didn't care. From where
I was standing, I could see the Parrish family cabin, where I spent one
of the best moments of my life there with Tenley, and then the most
painful when Jagger discovered our betrayal. It was a long time ago
and totally not relevant to what is happening in my life right now. I
carried it with me for years, and then I used it to not only hurt my best
friend but Tenley too when she returned home years later.

Before Jamie died, he asked me to bring him out here to look at
the water and feel the breeze coming off the mountains that would chill

our skin. I thought he was crazy and so did his parents, but I knew there would be no way of stopping Jamie once he set his mind to something. He was weaker by then but still managed to walk by just leaning on me. After he picked the spot, we sat down in silence. Long minutes turned into hours before he finally voiced a single word to me. While staring at the running water, the memory of that time hit me, and I was catapulted back to that day, here with Jamie.

"Shane, I'm not sure how much time I have left, so I'm going to say my peace, and then we will not speak of this again."

I said nothing, which is what he expected. He needed me to listen, so I did.

"You're lost, my friend. You're lost to loving Tenley and hurting our brother. You're so lost that you don't know what direction to walk in next, but that's where I come in. You are a good man, Shane Rhodes—one of the best—but that doesn't mean you are exempt from making mistakes. You made a foolish one with my sister; she knows that, and so do you, but it's one that can be repaired in time. I want you to know that I have taken steps to right that wrong and help not just my sister, but my brothers as well."

"Jamie, what does that mean?"

"Don't worry about it, you'll know when the time is right. Today is not that day. You need to get your life together and continue with the dream that we had as brothers. You'll never know how sorry I am that I will not be here with you to live it, but you and Jagger will."

"I don't see how, Jamie. I hurt him deeply."

"Yes, you did, but he will forgive you in time."

"In time? And how am I supposed to know how long that is?"

"You won't. It will happen when he's ready to tell you."

"And if he's not? Then where does that leave me in all of this?"

"Come on, Shane. Is it really that hard to figure out? You live. Right now, you feel as if you have lost everything you have ever cared about, but my friend, you would be wrong to believe that."

SHANE

I watched him struggle to get up, and once he did, he walked over to one of the huge trees that we had here on the ranch. He placed his two hands on it and felt the texture beneath.

"This oak is probably a hundred years old, maybe more. Its roots are buried miles beneath the earth with a strength that is so strong, there's nothing like it. Season to season, here it stands, to continue to grow and be strong." He continued to stare at the tree and then turned back to me. "You have the same strength in you, Shane, and it's that strength that will help you mourn me when I pass, and then repair your friendship with Jagger. It's the same strong roots that will help you build your own foundation for your future here on this ranch working side by side with our fathers and flourishing in the fact that your two hands built this beautiful land we are standing on right now. I need you to forgive. I need you to move on and not be trapped in the past, especially the painful parts. Do what I will no longer be able to do."

"What's that? Damn, you are beyond confusing."

"Live! Live, Shane, and don't take one God-given day for granted."

The memory of that conversation with Jamie hit me so hard in my heart that I couldn't see beyond my own tears. I may not have understood all that he was saying back then, but I sure as hell do now. It took me five long years to come to terms with what I did to Jagger and Tenley.

Next to Wendy, Shelby was the one person in my life who always believed in me and fought for us in more ways than I ever did. She remained by my side through the many months of therapy I endured after Jagger's accident. She told me that she loved me every single day, and when I pushed her away because I felt I wasn't good enough for her, she took me in her arms and never let go.

After I worked out my differences with Jagger and he finally forgave me, I felt free for the first time in a long time. Free to finally be able to give my heart—my whole heart—over to Shelby. She had never been happier more so than on the day of our wedding when she finally became mine. The memories of Shelby, Jamie, and my entire life here on this ranch came crashing down on me with such a force that it felt as if the earth had shifted and I was on solid ground again. I knew what I had to do.

As I wiped away the last of my falling tears, I began walking back to my truck, but not before something held me back. I turned and saw a ripple in the water, almost as if a stone just skipped over the clear waters. A cool breeze was felt on my face, and there was not one cloud in the sky above, just rays of sunshine casting a glow all around me.

"Thank you, Jamie. You're never too far away, are you? I love you, my brother, and miss you every single day. Take care of my son while I take care of his mother."

Another cool breeze hit me, and then I smiled up at the sky.

"Okay, I'm going. I'm going home."

The answers I was seeking yesterday would not be found in a bottle. No, I was wrong believing that. I was wrong to hurt my father, but being the man that he was, I knew he would forgive me. And I was wrong to leave my wife when deep inside she was begging me to stay.

A long time ago, I was blessed with forgiveness. I knew that act went both ways, just as much as I knew that I could no longer blame myself for the loss of our son. It had been the longest year of my life carrying the burden of that loss with me and almost succumbing to it. *We have to make us work, we just have to.*

I can't stand the fact that Shelby was thinking of hurting herself, but then again, I was doing the same thing. I used and abused alcohol every single time we fought, which was most of the time. When I was up on the mountain yesterday, I wasn't thinking clearly, not at all. I was reckless and irresponsible and not caring about anything or anyone. It could have been the same for Shelby when she was staring at the guns in the cabinet. One moment, one choice, had the power to change our lives forever. *No, that already happened, and as long as I'm breathing, I will never allow Shelby to ever believe taking her own life would be a good thing.*

My jaw still smarted a bit where my father hit me, a punch I surely deserved. I was better than the man he had to knock some common sense into yesterday, and I knew I could be better for Shelby. I held my hand over my heart and once more thanked every living soul in my life, along with the angel above that always had my back and never gave up on me.

As I made my way down the private road that would bring me home to my wife, I held onto the hope I found by the river. We would be stronger than the pain and find us again in the love we felt for one another. *It's there, I know it is, and once I am able to look into Shelby's eyes again, I'll know forever without a doubt that we will be okay.*

5

Hope is not lost

Shelby

I had been pacing back and forth waiting for Shane to come home to me, but I wasn't sure if he would. We had so much to work out in our marriage, and although he sat and listened to what I had to say, he still left anyway. This made me feel scared, because if he chose not to come home, I couldn't really say that I blamed him.

Where would we go from here? Divorce? It's unimaginable to come to terms with. I love Shane. He's the only man I want to spend my life with; I just hope it isn't too late. I looked down at my phone to see no messages. Of course, I would hear the alert if there were. *Should I call his father? Maybe Jagger and Tenley? I just don't know what to do, and I am beside myself with worry.*

"Damn, woman, you're going to wear down the hardwood floor if you keep that up."

I nearly jumped at the sound of his voice unexpectedly at the front door.

"Shane? Is it really you?"

He took his hat off and placed it down on the entryway table. Brushing his overgrown hair out of his eyes, he just smiled back at me.

"Yeah, darling, it's me. We're you expecting someone else?"

"Only you, cowboy." I said, holding back my tears of happiness. *He came home to me.*

I could barely remain standing on my two feet and rushed over to Shane for him to sweep me up in the best hug of my life. I held his face and just kissed him all over until I was breathless.

"Did you mean it?" he asked.

"What?" I questioned.

"Baby, you know what I am saying to you. Did you mean it? You want to try again and make our marriage work? You want to be my wife again? And I do mean in all areas of our marriage. I will not settle for anything less."

"With all my heart, Shane. I've been so cruel to you, and I am so very sorry for my behavior this past year. I love you so much, and you mean everything to me. You coming back means that you want to try again too? Right?"

He let out a deep sigh and continued to hold me in his arms. I thought he was going to put me down, but instead, he carried me upstairs to our bedroom, kicking the door closed behind him.

After he placed me on our bed, his intentions were clear; they always were when it came to Shane. In record time, he removed my clothes and all of his and then climbed back onto our bed, where his eyes were concentrated on mine.

"I love you, Shelby, and there is no one more important in my life than my wife. I've waited so long for you to come back to me, and now with your consent, I would like to make love to you and prove just how much I want you."

"Yes, Shane, please make love to me. Make me yours again in every way possible."

"Thank you, Shelby, because that's exactly what I intend to do."

My body was pulsing with anticipation. It was always like this with Shane. He was a force to be reckoned with and brought us to new heights every time we were together. He led, of course, and all I could do was submit over and over again until we both cried out our release. I think he tried to be gentle, but then his need to dominate and regain what he felt he lost was greater than tenderness at the moment. I was petite in frame and most times when Shane got like this, I felt him for days as he would ravage my insides with his hard, thick cock. It didn't matter, not today. We both needed to feel this, remember this, and take back what we had almost lost.

He tugged at my hair as his other hand held my hands. He didn't want to be touched, not yet at least. His expression was determined and hard as he rode out his release. He poured so much of himself inside of me that I was too full of his hot cum, and it began to seep out of me. When he finally disconnected from my body, he rolled over, taking me with him.

"Fuck me!" he barked out.

"You can go again?" I asked, shocking myself at the question.

"Yes, I can. Now ride me," he demanded.

His hands gripped hard into my hips as I pressed my palms onto his chest for support. He was relentless as he pumped harder and harder into me. I felt as if I was going to rip in two, but then with a roar of a scream, he came again, filling me once more. He held me in place for a moment and then sat straight up to wrap his arms around my waist. He inhaled me and kissed me all over.

"Thank you, baby," he said.

"Thank you?" I whispered. "Are you okay, Shane?"

"Never better."

He kissed me once more and then flipped us again, where I was on my side with Shane now spooning from behind me. He clicked the light off and told me to go to sleep. I was so full of him and wanted to clean up, but he would not let me, not even to move an inch.

He'd never been this possessive before, and I wasn't sure what to make of him right now, but I knew not to challenge him further. I would wait until he fell asleep and then would try to move from under his heavy limbs so I could clean up. I managed to get some sleep, but I was uncomfortable and finally got up from the bed. Shane was still out, probably still hungover from yesterday, and I knew he hadn't slept in days.

I was as quiet as I could be showering and changing into clean panties. We usually didn't sleep in much more than this, but I grabbed a short robe and was going to lay beside him when he began to toss and turn.

He looked in pain as if he was having a nightmare. He kept saying he was sorry and to stay. His words were my undoing as new tears began to fall down my face. Shane had carried so many burdens on his shoulders this past year, and not for one second had I allowed him to forget them. I soothed him as much as I could until his eyes flared open and he looked cornered in his distress.

"Shane, it's okay. I'm here."

"You were gone. Why did you leave?"

"Shane, I didn't go far, just took a shower. I'm here, baby. I'm here, and I'm not going anywhere."

He looked around the room and then back to me. He was drenched in sweat and looked scared. He reached for me and pulled me back into bed. With a forceful tug, he ripped away my panties and sunk deep inside of me, making me buck my hips forward. I was sore, so sore from the multiple times we made love, but I wasn't going to deny Shane of this connection he needed. He emptied his hot seed in me once more and then nearly collapsed from exhaustion.

Making love with Shane had always been at the level of "rock my world" type of sex, but tonight he was different. He'd never hurt me and didn't tonight, but if I was being honest with myself, he may have scared me a little.

He had a right to all of these feelings which I didn't consider and it drove a wedge between us. He held me close to his body and quickly fell back to sleep. He was restless a little, and then when I finally thought he was down for the night, I heard him mumble a few words. I listened as carefully as I could, and there was no mistaking what I heard.

"Don't leave me, Shelby. Whatever you do, just don't leave me again. I won't survive it."

I kissed him gently a few times and then I waited for his breathing to even, and I knew he was asleep. I brushed away his hair and stroked my fingers through it. For a hard-working, rugged cowboy, he sure does have soft hair.

I kissed him once more and made a silent promise to my husband. *"I will never leave you again, I promise you, Shane. I don't deserve you, and I know if I said these words to you aloud, you would silence me and tell me that wasn't true, but I know better. You are amazing, and throughout this year of pain and loss, I hurt you deeply, and that regret is on me, not you. You tried so hard to reach me, and I refused you at every turn. I'm so sorry to have done that to you and hope one day you will forgive me. I love you, Shane. We are going to make it, because I just don't see my life without you. Just be patient with me."*

I kissed my sleeping cowboy one more time, and he didn't stir a bit, which showed me how tired he was. I slept as close as I could and felt his warmth as sleep finally took me too.

6

Wrecked

Shane

She was sleeping so soundly that I didn't have the heart to wake her, so I crept out of our bedroom as quietly as I could and went downstairs to start the coffee. It was early enough for me to join the crew if I wanted to, but I wasn't ready to get back to my norm, or whatever the fuck that is.

If I wasn't totally throwing myself into work on the ranch, I was drowning in a bottle of whiskey. I had been so angry with my wife for punishing me for our son's death that that was the only emotion I knew how to feel.

Last night was a complete blur to me with Shelby asking me to come home so we can try to work on our marriage. That she was sorry and she loved me and wanted me as her husband again. *How the hell do I begin to absorb those words and move forward with my wife? Can I do that and just forget everything we've been through? Fuck! I don't know where to go from here.*

"What are you doing?" I said aloud to myself in frustration.

"Shane, are you okay?"

I didn't hear or notice Shelby standing behind me, and after last

49

night's nightmare, I couldn't begin the morning with another fight. I just couldn't do it. I let out a breath and turned to face her. She had her arms crossed over her chest with concerned eyes focused on me.

"I'm fine, baby. Nothing for you to worry about."

"Shane, I know it may not seem easy at first and I know it's going to take a lot of time to get back to where we were, but you can talk to me. I love you, and I'm here, Shane, and I promise I will never leave you again. Please tell me that you believe me?"

"Shelby, I…"

"Shane, I get it, I really do. I don't expect our life to just be perfect again or how it felt when we got married and all the wonderful that happened after. Take all the time you need, but please, if you can promise me anything, just please don't leave me. You said those seven words to me last night and when I promised you that I wouldn't, I meant it. So, I'm asking the same of you. I honestly don't know if I can survive another loss, so all that I am asking is that you take some time and think about what those words really mean not just for you, but for me too."

"Baby, I know and I'm not trying to hurt you here, but I just don't know what to say that's not going to come out wrong. I don't need any more time away from you, but I am feeling kind of confused right now and a little lost, if you want to know the truth."

"Truth works, and no matter how much you may think it will hurt me, the distance will hurt me more. I take full responsibility for my role in our problems. I am ashamed of that person, and I never want to be like her again. I'm so very sorry."

I took her in my arms and held her as close as I could. "Shelby, I don't want to hear one more apology come from your beautiful mouth. I can't take it, and I'm not sure you can either. I need a shower, and then I have to meet up with the guys. Can we talk later?"

"Of course, we can. Will you be gone all day?"

"Probably, I have some people that I need to see and a lot of fences to mend."

"They love you, Shane, and I do too. Can I pack you a lunch?"

"No, I'm good. I'll see you for dinner. If I'm going to be late, I'll call, okay?"

"Yup, no problem," she said, trying not to cry in front of me.

She began pulling out pots and pans and started breakfast as if it was just a normal morning for us. I felt horrible.

"Shelby, this is all that I'm capable of right now, but I'm not running, I promise you. I just need to clear my head, and the best way to do that is working the ranch. Please tell me that you understand that? This is not me rejecting you."

"I understand. Now get going before you lose the morning." She went back to preparing breakfast.

I decided not to say anything more and just went upstairs to shower. I called Jagger and asked if I could meet up with him sometime today, but his schedule was packed and he would have to see, so that left my father. I didn't need to call him, as I expected he was probably already waiting for me to show up. I parked my truck and kind of just stayed rooted in my seat, unable to move. I felt numb and not sure of what to do next.

"Are you going to sit there all day? Or are you going to chop some wood? He's out back waiting for you."

"Hi mom," I responded in a defeated tone.

All I could focus on was how Shelby looked when I left her standing in our kitchen this morning. Although I promised I would stay, leaving was leaving, and for all she knew, I may have left for good. My mind was just all mixed up right now, and I hated that I was throwing all these confusing signals at her.

"You okay, son?"

"No, not really, but I'm trying."

"Are you, Shane? Because it doesn't look like that from where I'm standing. You look so despondent, and it's just breaking my heart. I thought you going home was a step in the right direction for you and Shelby."

"Mama, it was, I guess, but now I'm not so sure. I need time to think, and I don't really believe that I can just forget the past year and act as if nothing has changed between me and my wife. Can I? Because it sure feels as if everyone in my life wants that."

"Shane, all we want is you back again. I know history cannot be rewritten, but you are the only one who can decide what today, tomorrow, and the next days will bring. Come on now, get going. I can't hold him off for too much longer. Your father is waiting."

I got out from my truck and took my mother in my arms for a warm embrace. She and my father were beyond wise and always guided me in the right direction, no matter if I wanted it or not.

I found him right where I knew he would be. He had split enough logs for two Wyoming winters.

"Hey, daddy, I'm sorry."

"Here, start chopping."

"Did you hear what I said?"

He took his ax and slammed it down onto the block. His features had hardened, but he kept steadfast in his stance.

"Did you hear what I said? This wood is not going to get chopped on its own, now get to it." He tossed me a pair of gloves and walked away.

Three hours later and many piles of wood chopped and stored, I was done. My shoulders were aching, and my muscles burned. Another life lesson on the books from Kip Rhodes.

"Dad, can I talk to you?"

"You know that you can, but I think we need to go for a ride."

"Okay, I'll bring my truck around."

"Not that kind of ride, son. Saddle up a horse, and let's go."

Yankee was at my house, so I chose to ride Bullet instead. He would definitely give me a workout. He loved the terrain, and once he was comfortable on the path, he usually took off like lightning.

We were out for about forty minutes or so, and then my father chose a spot that where the horses could rest and for us to talk.

"Dad, what are we doing up here? Are you going to give me another round of tough talk? Because I've heard it all before, and I'm not sure if I can handle anything else."

"You're lost," he said.

"What?"

"Don't stand there dumbstruck, boy! You are so lost that you cannot see straight. If it's not in the bottom of a bottle, you go catatonic and shut down. You have to rejoin the living, son, before we lose you too."

"I'm trying, dad. What do you want from me? I didn't have a clue as to what to say to you this morning, and I don't know now. You're right. Everyone is right. I am fucking lost and so far down in my own personal black hole that I'm not sure if I will be able to climb out. Here's the worst part: as much as I love my wife and want her healed and whole again, I'm so fucking angry with Shelby, and I just want to hit something really hard but get the free pass when I do. I don't need any more judgment or self-righteous advice. What I need is to go back to the moment when I decided that leaving on a scouting trip was a good idea, and not fucking go!"

"Well, that's a beginning. You need to talk to your wife, and it cannot be put off any longer. If you two stand a real shot at reconciliation, then you have to communicate with her and not just leave for parts unknown, sinking further down into that hole of yours. It's time, son, once and for all, to work this out. Because you're right about one thing: I'm not sure how much more you can take, and that goes double for my daughter-in-law."

"You know, dad, the last time we had a conversation like this, you punched me out, which I still feel."

"You deserved it. I promise I won't hit you again, but I will give you a hug, because it's what you need right now."

He took me into his strong arms and just allowed me the time to let my feelings out. When I was done, we rode the horses back to the stables, and then I left for home.

I wasn't sure what I would say once I got there, but I knew I couldn't avoid the much-needed heart-to-heart that I needed to have with my wife.

I looked up to the sky in hopes that Jamie would give me some kind of sign about what to do. I missed him so much, and if there were ever a time to send me some divine intervention, this moment would be it.

7

Hard truth

Shelby

After Shane left this morning for parts unknown, I just sat alone at the kitchen table, nursing the same cup of coffee for an hour without moving. I just sat there with no clue what to do next. I wanted to rush after him and beg him to stay, but I knew I could not do that.

Once I did get up, I took the hottest shower of my life to possibly wash away all the wrong that was between me and Shane. I knew I broke him first, then losing our son broke him again, and then blaming him for that loss completely destroyed him. He hadn't said the words to me, and maybe that was the problem standing between us. I was the one that put it all on him, and up until yesterday, I took zero responsibility for the accident and our son's death.

I knew what had to happen and it scared the hell out of me. He needed to say the words. He needed to claim it and make me own it, because if he didn't, then we truly had no chance at making us work again. I wiped away my tears and washed my face the minute I heard his truck pull up in front of the house.

"He's home, Shelby. He came home to you, so now go to him and tell him how much you love him. Be brave enough to face this head-on with your husband. You got this, Shelby. Just ask him the one question you never had the courage to ask him before today, and suck it up, no matter what he responds back to you. You've got this, Shelby. You are so strong, and you've been through a hell of a lot. Talking to your husband should be the easiest thing in the world to do. Now, go get him."

I gave myself the much-needed pep talk without knowing that Shane was standing off in the doorway, listening to every word I just said to bolster my confidence. *Where is a rock so I can crawl under it and die?*

"Shane, I didn't hear you come in," I said, flustered, stumbling over my words in embarrassment.

"Clearly." He bit his bottom lip trying to hold in his laughter.

"Shit! You heard me, didn't you?"

Shane actually held his stomach and laughed until he began wheezing. It was like he was having a fit or something pretty close to it, but it was also the happiest sound in the world. *Wow, I didn't know how much I missed this side of him. This right here was my Shane.*

"Okay, you can stop laughing now."

"Oh, I'm sorry, baby, but I needed that. Come here."

His arms were extended, and I just about leaped into them. He kissed me in between the last vestiges of his laughter and then held my face and placed kisses on my forehead.

"I love you. I needed to laugh before I..." He hesitated for a few beats, and then the rare happy look Shane had worn was gone and replaced with uncertainty. He said, "We need to talk, and this time I will tell you everything."

"It's late. Are you hungry?" I asked him before stepping out of his arms.

He shook his head no, and then I just decided to rip off the Band-Aid and give Shane the go-ahead to either heal...or break us forever. There was no in-between anymore.

"Whatever you have to say, just say it," I said.

"Come and sit with me, please."

I followed him into the living room, where earlier I had lit a fire. It was too tempting to sit by the fire, since it held so many memories of the two of us making love in front of it. I took a seat in the oversized chair, while Shane sat across from me on the sofa, a table separating us.

"Shelby, you know that I love you."

"And I love you."

"Well, that's good to know, but sometimes it's not enough."

"You're scaring me."

"I don't mean to, but I'm scared too, Shelby. It feels as if I have been in this mind-numbing fog for the past year, and it's cold, draining, and unforgiving. It drags me down and suffocates me at times. I fight to get out, and then I'm faced with another barrier that will not let me rise to the surface to break down the walls to where I'll be free. Free to return to the life I had before I said goodbye to you on that morning when the life we had just shattered and died on the side of the road."

His words were blades slicing me into shredded ribbons. I deserved this, and I was the one that asked him to tell me everything.

He said, "I shouldn't have made love to you last night. It was a mistake, and I was wrong to do that to you. I lost complete control and took what I wanted, never considering your feelings. I was still very drunk and at a low point in my life. I argued with my father, resulting in him hitting me and knocking me to the ground, where I stayed and drank some more. I never expected for you to say the words you did when I came home, and then I used those words for my own pleasure to ease the mountain of guilt that I have been carrying with me. For one fucking minute, I just wanted to feel something other than pain, and I took that out on you. I'm so sorry, baby, and sorrier if I hurt you in any way."

I rushed over to him and got down on my knees, taking his hands in mine. He looked distraught.

I could not have him taking anymore blame. "Listen to me. You did not hurt me. You did not use me. You would never do that. Even with the rawest emotions raging through you, I still believe you would exercise control and never push me further than I could handle. Please don't degrade what we shared last night, not when it meant so much to me to be that close to you again. Shane, for me, it felt like a new beginning."

He pulled back his hands as if my touch tainted him. He looked disgusted and got up and paced the room. "How could you say that? Dammit, Shelby, do you know me at all? Yes, our lovemaking has always been explosive, but it has never been laced with volatile emotion. And then I had a fucking nightmare that you had to witness."

"And? Don't you think I haven't had the same nightmare haunting me? I know I made a catastrophic mistake by getting behind the wheel even after you begged me to wait for the ambulance. I should have listened. I don't know why I allowed my panic to get the best of me. That accident changed my life—*our* life—together and ended all hope for us ever having any more children. That's on me, Shane, and I will no longer blame you. You have to say it. Tell me, Shane, please."

"Fine! I fucking blame you! You had time to wait, but you wouldn't listen to me and then you hung up, and I couldn't reach you. I couldn't reach anyone on that fateful day, and I was driving in the middle of nowhere with nothing to do but drive and hope I reached you in time. And then you just shut me out. You blamed me every single day for months, reminding me over and over again how I wasn't here for you and our son, and how I am the reason for his loss when we both know what happened to him was not my fault. Shelby, do you have any idea how much that hurt me? How much that literally destroyed every piece of me? It was not all at once either. It was a slow and painful torture that just ate away at me until you pushed me away again for the last time, resulting in me almost drinking myself to death up on that ridge."

"Shane, oh my god. I'm sorry. I'm so sorry."

"Stop saying that! I told you I can't stand to hear those words again. I know you're sorry, just as I have been, but does it matter at this point? It took my father reminding me that our son's death was something greater than that fucking accident. We had no way of knowing about the knots in his cord. We would have lost him no matter what, Shelby, and as sad as that would have been, we would have gotten through it together and tried again when we were ready. But you took that away from us by getting behind that wheel and driving recklessly on that day. So, yes, I fucking blame you for that choice just as much as you blame me for leaving on my trip."

He let out a deep breath and slammed the walls with his fists. I remained where I was just crying and reeling from every word he shouted at me. I knew I had hurt him but never realized how much. He gave me what I asked for, and it hurt like hell to sit here and relive it all again with Shane, something we have never done until now.

I got up off the floor and slowly walked over to him. His muscled back was hard as a rock with layers of tension. He didn't look at me, and I was unsure if I should touch him. Cautiously I walked closer and wrapped my arms around his waist.

He didn't push me away but still remained quiet. It was okay; he was giving me more than I deserved. I placed my cheek on his back and breathed him in. I held back my tears and whispered how much I loved him and didn't voice any more apologies, just whispers of love for my husband and hope that he would find it in his heart to forgive me.

"Shane, will you please turn around and look at me?"

He did without hesitation, and that's when I saw them. His eyes were filled with tears that were falling down his face. It wasn't often he showed this side to me, maybe not ever; cowboys don't cry. But he was more than that, he was my husband, and he was hurting right now.

I told him, "I love you, and I don't want you to feel bad for telling me the truth. It's what I asked for. You needed to do that, and now all I am hoping for is that you will try to find it in your heart to forgive me.

I want you, Shane, and our marriage. I will do anything to make us right again. All that I ask is for you not to leave and to work it out here with me. Can you do that?"

"I didn't believe you would want to after I told you the truth."

"I'm stronger than you think, and it took me a long time to finally admit the truth to myself and to come to terms with it all. Wendy helped me finally see the truth, and it was a hard pill to swallow, but I'm glad I did it, because it has brought us here together at this moment. I'm here, Shane, and I promise you with everything I have inside of me that I will never hurt you again and never push you away. I love you. I want you and our life together. Please, please, Shane, am I too late?"

8

Healed

Shane

Feeling the weight of the world suddenly lift away from my shoulders, I looked deeply into Shelby's eyes and whispered, "You're not too late. I may not know what tomorrow will bring, but I do know that I don't want to face it without you."

"Oh, Shane, I love you so much. Does this mean you forgive me? I mean really forgive me for everything I put you through?"

"Before today, I truly didn't know if I could, and then you challenged me to finally face the truth. For some reason, I could do it, when all the times before I shied away from talking to you in fear that you would run. So when I finally let it all out today, I think I'm still in shock that you stayed. I wasn't sure you would but then I walked through the door and saw you."

"Shane, no matter how much you screamed at me, I knew the truth finally needed to be voiced. I'm not angry, babe, just the opposite. I'm relieved that everything is out in the open now, and we can finally be honest with each other again. I am not naïve in believing that we can just skip over the past and behave as if everything is okay. I know it's going to take work and a lot of patience, but if I know we can be united on this subject, then I think it will make it easier for the both of us, don't you?"

"I agree. I love you, and I will not give up on us. If it's okay with you, I'd like to begin counseling again with Wendy. If you're not comfortable with her, then we could find someone else, but it's needed."

"Wendy is fine by me. I trust her completely."

"Okay, I'll give her a call in the morning to schedule a few appointments, and then we will see how it goes."

"Okay, sounds good. Um, Shane, may I ask you a question?"

"You can ask me anything," I replied and leaned in to give her a kiss.

"Will you make love to me?"

I literally felt a rush of exhilaration hearing her question. I wanted to scream "yes" at the top of my lungs, but I also believed we may not be ready to go there again. However, the look in her eyes was telling me different.

"I want to, believe me, but are you sure? Especially after today?"

"Absolutely sure. No matter what you believe, husband, I felt our connection last night as we made love, and I don't regret anything. If that was you unleashing some long overdue aggression, then I'm happy it was me that you took it out on. I know that may sound sadistic, but I don't care. You are my husband, and no matter how upset you are, I know in my heart that I am safe with you. I need you, Shane. I need to feel you inside of me again. I need everything. Please don't say no."

Without another word spoken, I lifted my girl into my arms and carried her upstairs to our bedroom and shut the rest of the world out. This time around, I took my time with my wife with slow and considerate intentions.

I removed her from her clothing as I allowed her to undress me too. I walked us into our huge shower and let the hot water spray down on us. She was loving as she gently caressed my skin with the plush sponge. I felt ripples of pleasure ignite through me as she began her descent to my lower region, making my dick come to life. I couldn't wait any longer, and it was like Shelby knew and dropped to her knees to take me deep into her mouth.

I shouted out an instant satisfied reaction but then quickly hoisted her up by her shoulders. I wanted to come inside of her, and it wouldn't be in her mouth. She easily wrapped her legs around my waist as I entered her with her back against the shower wall. This would be quick and rough and not what I had intended to begin our night with, but she wasn't complaining as she bit down hard on my shoulder and shouted my name.

I loved it when she was all worked up like this. She was happy and wanted this just as much as I did. I came so hard that my body was shaking while still holding up Shelby. When I finally placed her down, her knees went a little weak. She flashed a beautiful smile at me, and we began to wash up again before stepping out.

Once we were dried off, she simply put on a robe, and I put on a pair of boxers and sprawled out in front of the fireplace we had in our bedroom. I knew we had so much to talk about and we would, but for now, I just wanted to be here with Shelby and enjoy the moment we were having.

The robe didn't stay on long as I took her again, showing her how much she was wanted and loved, reassuring her that we would be okay. It was what I believed for the first time since losing our son, and although she didn't say the words, I knew she believed the same.

9

I hate therapy

Shane

After a few conversations with Wendy, she felt we would be better off talking with one of her colleagues who did not know us and who could offer a perspective that Wendy couldn't because of how close she was to us.

I wasn't happy about it, because I didn't trust too many people. After what Shelby and I had been through, we needed someone to truly be on our side, and that person was Wendy. She agreed to continue to counsel me one-on-one, but not as a couple. Shelby tried to calm my nerves and told me that everything would be alright, but I still had my reservations.

It had been a couple of weeks since our explosive reconciliation, and in that time, we talked every single day and caught up with each other with everything we missed as a couple over the past year. Yes, we were together and lived under the same roof, but we had lived as practical strangers constantly at war hurting each other because we could not move beyond our loss. Now, it was all changed, and we had a renewed purpose in our future.

Shelby squeezed my hand to reassure me, but I didn't want to be here at all. A few minutes later, a smart-looking woman probably in her early fifties walked out and greeted us. She was impeccably dressed, making me feel out of place with my standard jeans and cowboy boots. Shelby nudged me, and I finally rose from my seat to say hello.

"Mr. and Mrs. Rhodes, Hi, I'm Dr. Palmyra Whitfield, but let's cut the formalities. Just call me Myra. I tried 'pal' once, but then all my clients kept inviting me over for dinner and I gained too much weight."

I'm so out of here. Thank you, Wendy, I said quietly to myself.

"That was a joke, Mr. Rhodes. Please, follow me into my office, and we will talk."

Did the good doctor have the ability to read thoughts too? I'd rather chop wood for three more hours than have to sit here and listen to someone analyze my life. Shelby flashed me a look and then I remembered my promise to try.

I awkwardly laughed but reluctantly followed the comedic doctor. Once inside, she closed the door behind her and gestured for us to take a seat on the plush sofa as she took the chair in front of us.

"You look nervous, Mr. Rhodes. Are you?"

"No, nervous is the last emotion I'm feeling right now," I said as Shelby squeezed my hand.

"Very well, why don't you tell me the first then?"

"Excuse me?"

"You said nervousness was the last emotion you are currently feeling right now, so if that's the last, then I'm curious what the first is. I would like for you to tell me how you are feeling."

"I don't want to be here."

"Why is that?"

"Pretty simple: I don't want to be here."

"Again, why?"

"Shane..." Shelby cut in.

"No, Mrs. Rhodes, I would like for your husband to continue."

"It's been a long and hard year," I said.

"And?"

"And what? What do you want me to say here, lady?"

"You can start by giving me one straight answer as to why you are so uncomfortable. It's not as if you are not familiar with therapy. You've been attending counseling sessions with Wendy Manning for years now, so what's the issue?"

"I'm out of here." I got up to stand, and that's when Shelby reached for my arm and demanded for me to sit back down. I knew I had pissed her off. That would be the last thing I wanted to do, but this office seemed so fucking clinical. I felt as if I was under the microscope with all her questions.

"You're free to go if you want, but I believe that will defeat the purpose of couple's counseling. How about we finish today's session, and if you are still uncomfortable at the end of it, then by all means, don't come back? I have never forced therapy on anyone who doesn't want it, and I will not start now with you."

"Shane, will you stay? You promised to try."

I huffed in defeat and agreed.

"Now then, since you are my last appointment of the day, how about we start over? And I'll even consider this session a test run, free of charge."

"That's very generous of you, Dr. Whitfield. Thank you."

"My pleasure. Let's remove the formalities and make things as comfortable as we can. Please call me Myra, and if it's okay, may I call you Shelby and Shane?"

"Shane, is that okay?" asked Shelby, as she turned to look at me with her sweet eyes.

I felt like an asshole. The past few weeks had been so great with all the talking we'd been doing, and here I was, fighting the one thing I said I would do to repair our marriage.

"Yeah, babe, it's fine. I'm sorry." I cupped her face and gave her a gentle kiss on her lips and then turned back to Myra. "I'm sorry, Myra."

"No apologies necessary. Okay, let's begin. You mentioned a hard year; why don't you tell me about it?"

"I'm not sure if I can. It's a scary subject, and it makes me afraid."

"Of what, Shane?"

"Losing my wife."

"Oh, Shane, I'm right here."

"Yes, but you were gone for a long time, Shelby, and a few weeks of good will not erase a year's worth of bad. And by saying that—I don't mean to hurt you—it just is, and I'm scared. I'm scared of saying the wrong thing. I'm scared that if I do something out of step, it may trigger a bad feeling. I'm scared to work my ranch and fear that you're angry with me for it."

"Shelby, listening to Shane tick off a few reasons why he's reluctant to therapy, how does that make you feel? What are you feeling right now?"

"I agree with Shane about being scared. What he said is true. I pushed him away for a year. I was cruel with my use of words and actions. I basically checked out of our marriage and retreated to a dark place that I never believed I would be able to crawl out of. It took a very special person to make me realize that my actions had severe consequences. It was either get myself together or walk away from Shane forever. Once I was faced with the hard reality of those two choices, I knew how wrong I'd been and how much I'd hurt my husband."

I held Shelby's hand and squeezed it just enough to show her that she never had to worry about losing me, because I wasn't going anywhere. She brought my hand up to her lips and placed a soft kiss on my rough and calloused one. She asked me to allow her to finish. I nodded, and she continued to address the doctor's question.

"I understand being scared, because I'm scared too. I'm scared that with all the apologies I have said to Shane, that maybe deep down he may not believe me and trust what I say is real. What happened to me, happened to the both of us. I love my husband, and I want my marriage. I'm willing to put in the work if it means I get to have Shane."

"Okay, but allow me to add something to that. I understand your fear, and I understand Shane's, but it's not just about work for you as a couple, but also for you as individuals. Shane is continuing to counsel with Wendy, and you are more than welcome to come here on your own to speak freely with me or seek out someone else, but I cannot stress it enough that in all of this, you still need to put yourself first. If you don't, and he doesn't, then it will be extremely difficult to live as one. Okay, that's it for today. Believe it or not, we did make good progress."

We left Myra's office feeling completely exhausted, but in the end, we agreed to continue with couple's therapy. Shelby signed on for individual sessions there, while I worked with Wendy.

Later that night while in bed, I did my best to communicate what I wanted to say to my wife. "Shelby, I'm really sorry about today. I behaved badly, and hurting you was not part of the plan. I thought I was ready, and then I sat down and felt the walls closing in on me. I freaked. I just want to move forward, but I know we have more talking to do before we can do that."

"Shane, we have already made positive strides to moving forward. We're here, right? Sharing our bed together, making love because it's where our hearts are leading us to, and not doing it because there's a void to fill."

"I would never use you, Shelby, I hope you know that. I want to possess you in every possible way, because you want me too. I'm scared of losing you. I'm scared of all the things we wanted for our family, and now we don't have them. I don't know how to separate and compartmentalize all these feelings I have."

"It's the same for me, babe, maybe more because I carried him for seven months. He was a part of me, and when I woke up in that recovery room, I immediately felt my stomach and knew he was gone. The emptiness was overwhelming. That was the beginning of the dark hole I fell into. I blamed you and exonerated myself. It wasn't fair to you. I pray that talking it out with Myra and Wendy and talking now like we are will get us to a place where we will not be so scared and those hopelessness feelings will be replaced with happy ones. Ones that we deserve. Shane Rhodes, you are worth it, and so am I. I promise I will try with everything I have to fight for us."

I let out a deep sigh and wanted nothing more than to lose myself in my wife, but I needed to share one more truth. "After I was told that our son had died, I was beside myself with grief. I was barely holding on and then Dr. Tillman asked me if I wanted to see him. I couldn't do it, Shelby, especially not without you."

"You never told me that. Why now?"

"I wanted to be honest and didn't want any unsaid words between us."

"I know you don't want to hear any more apologies from me, but I am so sorry for leaving you all alone when I should have been there for you. I'm here now and for you to give me another chance means so much. I promise that I will not hurt you or retreat to a dark place that you can't reach me again. I love you, Shane."

"I'll never stop loving you, Shelby. We are going to make it, I promise you."

"I know."

I was done with talking and flicked off the light while wrapping my wife around me. This day had totally sucked, but while I made love to Shelby, I promised her that tomorrow would be better. It just had to be.

10

The road back to us

Shelby

It had been nearly a month seeing Dr. Whitfield as a couple, along with Shane having one-on-one sessions with Wendy. They were unbelievably close, and he trusted her a great deal. I only made two individual sessions with Myra and decided that I felt more comfortable with Shane beside me than on my own.

I tried to reason the fact that what I would discuss with Myra would ultimately benefit my relationship with Shane, but I couldn't help but feel as if I was also betraying him in a sort of way. We needed to be on the same page as a couple, and I truly felt that if we could repair what was broken between us, then I would be fine. Slowly but surely, we were getting there.

The sessions that followed our first meet and greet were establishing who we were and reaching the goals of who we were before losing our son and what would it take to get there again. We both knew it could never be the same more so standing on solid ground.

Myra took turns hitting us both with the tough questions, and today, like all the other times before, she did not hold back. Her aim was at Shane, and every time he squeezed my hand, I was afraid he might have reached his breaking point and throw his hands into the air before walking out on therapy and me. He didn't though and just sat through it.

Although the question was for him, it hit me straight in my heart. "Shane, we've talked about your child. Yours with Shelby, and he's always referred to as son, child, and baby. Did you name him?"

I watched Shane take a deep breath, and his features hardened. I knew what he would say, and this was just another moment of truth for him to reveal.

"Yes, we did."

"And? May I know it?"

"I'm not sure I can do that, at least not right now."

"Why not, Shane? Perhaps vocalizing his name will release some of the torment you and Shelby feel over his loss."

"I don't see it that way, not at all. You see, with Shelby getting injured in the accident and taking all those months to recover, I had to make decisions that were not just mine to make but had to at the present time. Shelby was in no shape physically or mentally to do so, and it all fell down on me."

"How did that make you feel, knowing it was all on you, where if the accident hadn't occurred, you probably would have made those decisions together?"

"It wasn't a good time. I was a wreck and so lost inside that I never knew what each new day would bring. I hated those days with every fiber of my being, and I hated that I grieved alone."

"Shelby, what about you? Did you grieve alone?"

"Every single day. I couldn't share what I was feeling. It felt as if I was buried under layers of pain and I couldn't break free from it."

"What about now?"

"Now, it's better. I'm not hiding from Shane, and when I have a bad moment, I share my feelings with him instead of running or pushing him away."

"That's a step in the right direction for the both of you. Okay, so now let's go back to my original question: May I know your son's name?"

"Why do you need to know? He was our son, not yours, and knowing his name is not going to change the fact that he's gone."

"Yes, that's true, but saying the words aloud may indeed help you. Isn't that why we are here? You must come to terms with his loss before you move forward with your life. Honestly, I don't believe you have crossed that threshold as individuals nor as a couple. Saying his name is a freeing exercise. It's a matter of acceptance. It's just like visiting his grave. Although you know he's not there, it serves as a place for reflection. A place you can visit and talk to him. Care to try? Shane?"

"No, I'm not ready."

"Very well. We can revisit when you are."

I felt sick to my stomach, and I knew he didn't feel all that better. On the way home to the ranch, I suggested we stop at the cemetery to visit our son's resting place. I didn't know back then that Shane and his family had plots near each other, so the first time going there, I discovered he was buried very close to James "Jamie" Fairchild. How could he not? He was Shane's best friend next to Jagger, and knowing Shane, he would want his brother in life watching over him.

Shane took the turn off the road that would lead to the cemetery, the sacred ground where our little boy eternally slept. He remained quiet as he held my hand climbing the steep hill. Once we reached the top, I was surrounded by the breathtaking view of King Mountain. I had been up here several times with our family and friends but never with Shane until today.

"It's beautiful up here, Shane. You chose a beautiful spot for our son," I said.

Still I was met with silence. He let go of my hand and dropped to his knees in front of the huge heart headstone with a teddy bear attached to its side and footprints etched on the front. I didn't know for the longest time until Wendy revealed to me that the footprints were of our son that Shane had used from the death certificate.

"It's beautiful, Shane. I would have never been able to do what you did, and I don't believe I ever said thank you. So, thank you for doing something I couldn't."

I watched his shoulders slump a bit, and then ever so slowly he traced the inscription with his finger and softly whispered what it said. He was so quiet that even though he was saying the words, they were not meant for me to hear.

Heaven will hold you before we do and keep you safe until we come home to you.
In loving memory for our boy, Ryder Shane Rhodes

"Ryder Shane Rhodes. There, I said his name," he said.

I tried to touch him, but he pulled away and walked away from me. He didn't go far, just to Jamie's grave and sat down on the bench that was placed in front of it. I said my prayers for our son and placed a kiss on his stone before walking over to Shane.

"Do you want to be alone? I can walk down by myself and wait for you, if that's what you want."

"No, Shelby, it's not what I want. I never wanted any of this. I'm trying here, I really am, but I don't feel fucking better saying his name. I want him here with us. I wanted to watch you with him, and I wanted to be his dad and teach him everything, but he died before we had all those things with him, and I'm angry. I'm angry because you grieved, I grieved, but we never grieved together. I grieved over all those gifts we were never able to bestow on him, and I feel cheated. I wanted him so much. Why did he have to die?"

"I don't know, Shane. I honestly don't know. People say some children are just not meant for this world but are needed in God's kingdom. I'm not sure if I believe that, but my mother has certainly told me that over and over again. I stopped fighting her and just agreed with her in the end just so she would stop talking about the predisposed destiny we all seem to have. I'm sorry I took our chance away from having any more children."

"No more apologies. Didn't we decide on that already?"

"We did, but I still feel I need to say the words. At least until you believe me."

He got up, faced me, and then cupped my face in his hands and placed a kiss on my lips that I needed to pay attention to feel. Once he broke the connection, he kissed me again, further deepening the message he wanted to express. "I don't blame you, at least not anymore. It's the truth, Shelby. My truth. I. Do. Not. Blame. You. And we don't need any more apologies, okay?"

"Okay."

We walked back over to Ryder's grave and held each other in a warm embrace. We stood there for a long time, and then we made our way down the hill and back home. Later that night, Shane continued to hold me in our bed as he whispered how much he loved me and promised that we would be okay.

What he voiced next took me by surprise, but I wasn't as shocked as I might have been six months ago. We had come so far in rebuilding our life together, and this was Shane finally voicing what he wanted. "I want to be a father."

His arms tightened around my body as he waited for me to react to his bold statement, but I was still replaying the six words over in my head. *"I want to be a father."*

"Shelby, I never believed I would ever ask you this, but what about the harvested eggs? Do you think we could try? I know it's completely insane considering we've only just started repairing our marriage and what the last year has cost us, but even acknowledging that truth will not stop me from at least exploring our options."

"Shane, are you sure? Because we would only have—maybe, at best—two attempts of a successful procedure with a surrogate, and if it fails, then it would be another devastating loss for us to go through again."

"Yes, it would be hard, but why did we harvest your eggs in the first place? We were being cautious back then for no other reason, and then the unthinkable happened and destroyed any chance of you conceiving another child. That miracle is just waiting to come to life. Please say something."

"Yes, I'll try but on one condition."

"Anything, just name it."

"Please promise me that no matter what happens, good or bad, we won't allow it to break us?"

"Baby, I promise with all my heart. I love you. Thank you," I said and held my wife in my arms as close as I could.

11

Falling into place

Shane

"Are you serious right now?" asked my father as I began to explain how Shelby and I would have a child.

"As a heart attack, dad. A long while back Shelby had frozen her eggs because with her mom and grandmother both being breast cancer survivors, she didn't want to take any chances. I thought at the time she may have been overreacting with her worry, but then I was on board with it. We did the procedure, and honestly, I placed it in the back of my mind and didn't think of it again until last night."

"Son, this is a life-changing decision for you two to take on. Are you sure you want to do this right now?"

"Daddy, what do you want me to say? No? Because you know how much I want to be a father, and now it's within reach of happening? Yes, I want to do this with my wife. Once we find a surrogate, we can begin the process."

"Shane, please reconsider, at least for the time being. You and Shelby have barely moved past the walking on eggshells stage, and now you just want to jump headfirst into parenting. This is very big.

You need to be sure."

"I am sure! Forget I even mentioned it." I threw my gloves down and stormed off toward the barn. "You can have Luke help you with the rest. I'm going for a ride."

"Shane, come back here. Shane!" he called out, but I ignored him and saddled up my horse to clear my head.

"Come on, Yankee. Let's fly for a bit." I gave my horse his command, and we took off for my favorite trail. Once we finally reached the pond, I rested Yankee for a bit. I tossed him an apple to nibble on, and then I walked over to the water's edge to skip some stones across the calm water.

"Fuck! Why does everything have to be complicated in my life?" I asked aloud with no one in sight to answer me back. Storming off was the wrong thing to do, especially having done that to my father, but he pissed me off. I thought I would be given support on this and not the reserved reaction he gave me. Maybe it was too soon to be doing this, but I couldn't help dreaming about it last night once we finally fell asleep.

I made my way back to the barn where I kept Yankee, and Luke and Wade along with a few ranch hands were laughing. I handed off Yankee and then asked what the big joke was. "Last time I checked, boys, you were still on the clock."

"Cool your jets, boss man. Everything is done. Wade was just telling us about the ghost we now have here in the barn."

"Ghost? What are you fools talking about?" I said as I hung up my saddle.

"Wade thinks we have a ghost here in the barn."

"Oh yeah? And what makes you think that?"

"Okay, laugh all you want, but the last three nights I have been awakened by some noise out here, and every time I come out to look around, it suddenly stops. I check all the horses and make sure everything is secure before closing the doors. I swear it's just a feeling, but it's like someone is watching me when I'm in here."

"Okay, fun time is over," I said as I made my guys go back to work.

"I'm telling you, boss, something is not right."

"Goodbye, Wade. Get down to the cabins and make sure the checklist is complete. We have campers arriving soon, and I want everything to be perfect."

"You got it," he said, leaving me in the barn alone.

"Ghosts! They're nuts," I said aloud to myself.

"Talking to yourself again?" I heard her say behind me. It was Shelby.

"Hey, baby, where did you come from?"

"The main house. I just dropped off a pie for Connie and Brock."

"That was thoughtful of you, I'm sure they appreciate it."

"I hope so. This making amends thing is hard."

"Baby, you never have to worry about that. Everyone here loves you, but no more than me."

"Well, that's good to hear. So, I thought you were working with your dad today? Where is he?"

"I don't know. We got into it, and then I got pissed and did what I do best."

"You took off?" she almost winced as she said the words.

"More like cooling off on my horse."

"Feel better?"

"No, but I'll get over it."

"Shane, are you about done for today?"

"Yeah, just about. I have some paperwork to do, but that can wait until tomorrow. The crew is down at the cabins making sure everything is set for next week."

"Great. I love when we get guests. Keeps us busy around here, that's for sure."

"Hey, Shelby, do you still want to be in charge of the reservations? I know you've enjoyed it in the past, but I didn't want to presume anything until I asked you first."

"Yes, of course, I want to help. I was actually down there myself this morning after you left for work. The cabins look great. The new supplies we ordered were delivered, and cabins one through six are now stocked up with everything the guests requested and then some. I'm on top of it."

"Wow! You never cease to surprise me. Thank you for that."

"It's what I signed up for, and I have to say I missed it. I even cleaned my office."

"As if it was a mess in the first place."

"No, just cobwebs from my absence. I swear to you, Shane, I'm okay and ready to work beside you again and do my part."

"That's music to my ears. I love you."

"I love you too. How about we go christen one of the new beds?"

"Don't even think about it."

"Okay, the wall then. Let's go."

I swooped in and put Shelby on my shoulder as she laughed and giggled all the way to the truck.

The following week, we had our much-anticipated appointment with our doctor. We were both so nervous and waited patiently while he read over our file. Our hands were linked together, and I think we were both holding our breath.

He closed the file and sadly smiled back at us. I knew at that moment whatever he was about to tell us would not be good.

"Okay, this is what we know," Dr. Tillman began to explain as Shelby covered my hand with hers. "Shelby, Shane, I'm sorry, but none of your eggs are viable."

"Did we wait too long?" asked Shelby.

"Yes. The longer the process is delayed, the chances of the embryo taking significantly decreases. At best, we were looking at a 2 to 12% success rate."

"What kind of odds is that? You had over 20 eggs, and not one was viable? What the fuck!" I shouted back at Dr. Tillman, who allowed me the room to vent my frustrations.

"Shane, please sit back down." My wife tried to calm me, but I couldn't look at her because of the immediate guilt I felt. I pushed her to do this, and now I felt as if I was breaking her heart all over again. She felt it, she always did. She got up and joined me over by the window, placing her arms around my waist. "Shane, I'm okay. I knew the chances and should have prepared you better, but you were so happy that I couldn't take your smiles away from you."

I turned around and held her face in my hands so she could look up at me. Her eyes always showed me what I needed to see. "And what about *your* smiles? This is just not about me. I feel another part of us has died, and our hopes of ever becoming parents are just fading away right before us."

"Shane, Shelby, hope is not lost. You could use a donor egg along with a surrogate. Your dream is not over, not by a long shot. Why don't you take some of this literature I have here and read up on it? Then when you're ready to talk about it, I'll be here."

Shelby took the papers, and then I apologized for my outburst.

"Not necessary, but thank you," Dr. Tillman responded.

"How are you feeling right now?" I asked Shelby as we drove away from Dr. Tillman's office.

"A little numb, but it will pass."

"Shelby, I didn't know this would happen. I never believed it was even a possibility. I shouldn't have gotten our hopes up."

"You didn't. How can I explain this without sounding as if I don't feel the same way you are right now? It's disappointing, yes, but nowhere near what we've already gone through. For seven months, I carried a baby inside of my body. I felt him move and watched my body change as he continued to grow, and then one day, he was gone and a huge piece of my heart died along with him. Making the decision to extract my eggs was almost a knee-jerk decision that I was pressured into doing because of my family's history. I told my mother that I wasn't ready for something like that, and then I found myself telling you that it was a good idea to do it, and then it was done. You just went along and supported that decision and never questioned me about it. I thought, wow, he's so wonderful to go along with this."

"What would you have had me say? Tell you no? Because I wouldn't have done that. I listened to your mom and you go on and on about the positive reasons why it was a good idea, and I saw it on your face. You were sure, so I was sure. In my wildest dreams, I never believed we would use those eggs because…"

"Finish that sentence, please."

"I never worried, because we got pregnant. I didn't want to worry about cancer that you may never get in your lifetime."

"Okay, that's honest. So, where do we go from here?"

"We keep moving forward and love each other. I can't live without you, Shelby, and as long as I have you, then the rest of it doesn't matter."

"Are you sure that I'm enough? We are enough?"

"I've never been surer. You and me, just us two."

That night my sleep was restless, probably a combination of the bad news from the doctor as well as the anxiety of the guests arriving the next day.

"Hey, taking off already? It's barely five," she called out the next morning.

"Don't remind me, but it's ranch life, and it's not going to run by itself."

"Can I make you some breakfast before you leave?"

"I'm going to run down to the cabins and do a final inspection before our guests arrive, check-in with the crew, and then I'll be back."

"Sounds good. I'll be here waiting for you."

I was almost skipping down to my truck, knowing how true that was. I had just finished checking all six cabins that were booked and was about to head home when I noticed something off with one of the vacant ones.

The door was open just enough for me to notice. I grabbed my shotgun from the truck, not knowing what would be waiting for me behind the door. This was Wyoming, and it wouldn't be the first time I came up against a bear. I slowly opened the door, and everything looked in order until I heard a noise coming from the bedroom. I cocked my gun and was ready for anything. I flew open the door only to find the window open and whoever had been here was now gone.

After I was finished looking around, all I found was food missing from the cupboards, and the extra comforter that was kept in the wardrobe was missing. I stowed my gun back into the truck and then called Wade and Luke to meet me down here.

"Hey, boss man, what's up?"

"Yeah, I think I found your ghost," I said.

"No shit! Where are you?"

"I'm down at cabin twelve."

"Okay, we're on our way."

12

Surprise guest...

Shelby

"How about we get some lunch? I'm over inventory," Tenley said and then plopped down on the couch.

"Come on, girl. I promised Shane I would have this done by today, and the clock is ticking."

"You know I have a law degree, right? Inventory is below my pay grade." She smiled as she kicked her feet up on my desk.

"You snob!" I laughed. "And I have a business degree and an overgrown bear of a husband that will skin me alive if I don't get this done."

"Maybe that's what you want."

"Slut!"

"Right back at you! You sound happy, Shelby."

"I am, we both are. After everything we've been through and then surviving our disastrous appointment with Dr. Tillman, we're still standing and in a very good place. Getting back to work is definitely keeping my mind busy and Shane's."

"You make a good team. You always did."

"Yeah, I think you and I both did pretty well in the husband department."

"Speaking of which, Jagger is waiting for me."

"Tenley, can you wait a sec?" I asked her.

"Sure, what's up?"

"I just want to say thank you for your friendship. I don't know what I would have done without you and Jagger. I pushed you away more times than I'm ashamed to admit, and you pushed back and stayed. I'm not sure if 'thank you' is even the right word, but it's how I feel. I'm just thankful for you both."

"We love you, Shelby. You are part of our family, no matter what."

"I miss my godson. Do you think we can have a day soon?"

"Absolutely, and he misses you too. We just didn't want…"

"I know, but I promise I'm fine and will continue to be fine."

After Tenley left, Shane arrived. "Hey, baby, are you ready?"

"Yes, I am, thank goodness, but…"

"But what?" he furrowed his brow.

"Are the guys breaking in here at night? I understand cowboys and their big appetites, but this is getting ridiculous. I didn't want to say anything, but when I did inventory, I noticed the quantity coming up short, and now it's happened again. I thought it was me at first, so I checked and re-checked my ordering, but it's right, Shane. So, if the ranch hands are not feasting at night, then we have a serious theft problem here."

"Okay, don't freak out, but we have a squatter on the property. I discovered it today while I was checking the cabins. I thought it might be a wild animal that got in, but clearly, someone has been sneaking in and using cabin twelve for shelter and knows where we store our supplies. I checked all the surveillance footage and came up with nothing. I don't know who it is, but I'm going to catch him and make sure he never comes onto this ranch again."

"Shane, how on earth can someone just bypass all our security and waltz onto our property like no one's business?"

"He must be pretty smart, that's for sure, but he has stolen from us for the last time, because I'm going to catch him."

"Have you told Brock or Jagger?"

"No, only Luke and Wade know so far. At least the ghost theory can stop now. Let's go home. My dad is waiting for us, and then I will deal with the squatter issue later."

Back at home and a few hours later, my father-in-law patted his stomach, making me feel proud that I could do something nice for him.

"That dinner was delicious."

"Why, thank you, Kip, always happy to have you over to our home."

"How is my son? He didn't say much to me tonight."

"You two are so alike, it's scary. He loves you, Kip, and respects you so much."

"I know he does. It's just sometimes I don't always know the right words to say to him without Shane blowing up at me."

"And for that, I'm sorry," Shane said from behind me.

"Hey, I didn't know you were standing there. I best be going. Thanks, darling, for supper."

"Anytime, Kip. Please give my best to Kathleen."

"I'll walk you out," Shane said.

I watched two very stubborn cowboys embrace and then walk out, laughing over something Kip had said. Man, I loved them very much and felt so lucky to have them both in my life. A few hours later, Shane was filling his pack with supplies.

"Are you going to be okay out there alone?" I asked.

"I'll be fine, sweetheart. You don't have to worry about me. Thank you for inviting my dad over here tonight. You're right, as usual."

"You just needed a push. He loves you, Shane, and would move heaven and earth for you if he could. He's a good man."

"Yes, he is, and I'm damn proud to be his son. All I ever wanted was to emulate him in every way possible. He's my hero and has never disappointed me, not ever. Everything I am is because of him, and I so wanted to pass those values down to our kids. Please tell me that dream is not over for us. We can adopt. I don't care if we have to travel the world to find him or her, but please just tell me that we both still have hope. It's all I need."

Shane's eyes were hypnotizing to the point that I was high and all on Shane Rhodes. I loved him so much at this moment that I just couldn't articulate the right words I wanted to say, so I just kissed him as passionately as I could manage. His hand caressed my back until he grabbed my ass, and before I knew it, my legs were wrapped around his waist.

"Please, babe, I need to see you," he whispered.

"Yes, Shane, take me right here."

I was wearing a skirt, which gave Shane easy access to tug once on my panties and successfully rip them. Before I could blink, he was buried deep in my wet folds, pounding his hard cock deep into my body. My walls clenched around him until I was screaming his name. We were both so close to losing our minds, and then Shane picked up the pace and continued to slam into me until he came so hard he barely remained on his feet.

"God, I fucking love you," he breathily said while kissing me all over my face.

"I love you too, cowboy, so much"

"Let me carry you upstairs."

"Shane, you're still in me. How are you going to do that?"

"Oh, baby, you wound me. Let's just say you bring out the wild animal in me." And with that encouragement, Shane made love to me again. I don't know where he gets his energy from considering the hours he works on the ranch. I asked him right before I literally passed out from exhaustion. He smiled and pulled me closer to his chest to hold me. My eyes were just about to close when he began to speak.

"I'm making up for lost time with you. You are my world, Shelby Rhodes, and I'm going to love you to the end of time."

SHANE

I tightened my arms around his waist and kissed his chest. He's right, we did lose so much time when we were grieving and struggling through our pain, but that's over now. He never gave up even though he probably should have. Shane being here and loving me the way he does is just one more reason I will do everything and anything in my power to make him happy.

I knew he had to leave to search for the squatter, but I just wanted a few more minutes with him. I asked Shane if he could wait until I fell asleep. He smiled and said he would knowing it would take but a minute or so. I knew once my eyes closed I would be fast asleep. I didn't feel the bed move when he left but that's okay. I knew he would be home soon and here with me.

13

Not at all what we thought

Shane

D amn, it was cold tonight. The weather shifted the last few days, and the nights here were getting increasingly colder, which meant snow was coming and it was going to be brutal. I was happy to get a head start on the winterizing of all the cabins. Reservations were booked out for the entire season.

I guess I understood why certain foods had gone missing along with the blankets. The person in question hiding out here on the ranch had to be homeless and probably in need of help, which I would have no problem providing.

I parked my truck out of the way and hiked on foot back to the cabins. I set up the cameras on each of the four trees that surrounded the area of the cabins, and then I climbed up high and positioned myself on the huge tree limb I hoped would hold me. It had been a while since I tree climbed, and it was always with Jagger and Jamie. I had to admit this was kind of boring just being here by myself.

About two hours in, I was about to call it for the night when I saw from my phone some movement on the cam near cabin twelve, the very same that was broken into. All our equipment was state of the art, but our mystery guest was not what I expected at all. The figure was small—ridiculously small—which puzzled me even more than I was when I began this crazy night. I climbed down the tall oak and made my way over to the cabin, trying carefully not to make a sound.

I knew the doors were locked, because I secured them all this afternoon, but I purposely left the window unlocked since this was his choice of entry. I slowly raised the window and climbed inside. This cabin was geared for a family size of at least four to six members, which made it bigger than the other units. Judging by the room décor, I was in the third bedroom of the cabin. I checked the closet, and it was empty. This was one level, so once I made my way out of this room, I would come face-to-face with the intruder. I had my gun ready just in case.

I entered the main living space and looked around with no one in view. "Shit, where are you?" I said as I lowered my weapon. Suddenly I saw movement coming from my peripheral vision, and I made a run after him.

"Hey, stop!" I called out, but he kept running. I chased him to the end of cabin row and then lost sight of him again. I looked all around and then one of the bushes moved, and I knew I had him cornered. I kept my gun secured and stepped closer to the dense brush.

"Okay, I am not going to hurt you, but you need to come out right now, or I will come in after you, and you won't like it if I do."

I counted to ten, and then I was going to pounce. I'd had enough of this game, and I was freezing out here. I stepped closer to the bushes, and what I found totally shocked me. It was a small boy, couldn't have been any older than seven years old, maybe eight. He looked so scared and small, crouching down beneath the branches.

"Hey, my name is Shane. I'm sorry if I scared you back there, but I promise you are safe. Can you come out of there for me?" I asked soft enough where I hoped he wouldn't be scared of me.

He nodded, which was good enough for me, and then I extended my hand out to him. Again, it was so small in my huge man hand.

"There you go."

He held my hand while I led us back to the cabin. I wanted to make sure he wasn't hurt from hiding in the bushes. Once inside, he ran to one of the bedrooms. I followed him and saw that he was clutching a small backpack to his chest.

"It's okay, son. Please let me help you. Are you hurt?"

He nodded no.

"Okay, can you come out into the living room with me?"

He shook his head no, so I took a knee to the floor and waited to see what he would do next. Minutes ticked by at a slow pace. I wasn't sure how long we were going to have this face off with each other. I tried once more to get through to him.

"I told you my name, remember? It's Shane. Can you tell me yours?"

Again, he shook his head no.

"Okay, are you hungry? Thirsty? Because I am, and I live in the big house up that road." I pointed in the direction of the window that faced the road where I parked my truck. I knew it was pitch black outside with only the moon to serve as our guide, but I had no idea what I was doing with this kid. I knew not to make any sudden moves that might scare him.

"So, how about you come with me and meet my wife who makes a delicious cup of hot chocolate? She counts out the marshmallows too!"

He slightly smiled, and I hoped it was enough to get him to trust me. He reached for my hand, and I slowly got up off the floor and began walking toward the door. I locked up the cabin, and then without giving him a choice I picked him up and carried him all the way to my truck. I placed him in the back and secured him in place. He was small but didn't appear to be hurt in anyway.

Shelby must have heard my truck pull up and came outside to greet me. It was so late and she should be in bed where I left her, but I secretly love the fact that she's not. Her bright eyes widened once she saw the little body that had fallen asleep, which I was now carrying inside. She covered her mouth in dismay and then followed me into our home. She grabbed a warm throw blanket we kept on the chair to cover his small body as I gently placed him down on the couch.

He must have been exhausted or so scared from fear about what I might do up in the cabin that he just passed out. I took my boots off to prevent making noise on the hardwood floors and had Shelby follow me out of the living room to the hallway, where I still had eyes on him.

In a whisper, she asked, "Shane, what's going on here?"

"That right there is our mystery squatter who's been seeking shelter on our ranch and taking what he could from going hungry. After I set up the cameras around the cabins, I waited and could not be more surprised when I saw his little body appear on the feed. All I could see was an illuminated figure, small but I didn't know until he took off and I had him cornered out in the bushes. Shelby, I had my gun with me. Holy hell! What if I had shot him?"

"You would have never done that, so don't even allow your mind to go there. You are an expert marksman and would not just carelessly disarm your weapon."

"I'd like to believe that was true in any circumstance I faced, but babe, I didn't know what was out there. I couldn't believe my eyes when I saw it was just a little boy."

"Where do you think he came from? I mean, Shane, we don't have a neighbor in sight for miles and miles, and although this ranch is well-developed, it still has parts that are rugged mountain terrain."

"No need to remind me, I've been working this ranch since I was a boy, probably around his age. I just don't understand it. He's so little. Where is his family? I haven't heard of any missing children, especially in this area."

"Okay, we both have so many questions, but none of them will get answered until he wakes up and hopefully can tell us who he is. Let me go fix him something to eat so it will be ready for him."

"Can you make hot chocolate? That was what got him to trust me enough to come home with me."

"Magic weapon, of course."

"Extra marshmallows too."

"That's a given. I'll be right back."

As I kept a watchful eye on the little boy who was still asleep on our couch, I made a call to Luke and Wade and filled them in on what was going on. They couldn't believe what I told them. They weren't expecting to hear that a little boy was the intruder. I told them to keep this quiet for now until I called my father, Brock, and then the sheriff.

"Is he still asleep?" Shelby asked as she came back into the living room.

"Yeah, he's out like a light."

"Shane, how do you think he got here? And how did he do it?"

"Beats me, babe, but hopefully once I call the sheriff he can tell me if there are any children who have been reported missing. I haven't heard of any, but you never know. We live so far away from everyone, I can't imagine how he pulled it off and in the elements. It gets pretty cold here at night, and what he's wearing is not nearly warm enough."

"Well, he was smart enough to take a blanket and pick the food he knew he could eat."

"Yeah, something tells me this little guy has been through a lot. Stay with him, will you? I'm going to go into the office to call Tenley. She knows a lot of people and probably can help us figure out what to do."

"Okay, go make your calls. We'll be fine."

I kissed my wife on her forehead and made my way down the hall and into the office, where I closed the door behind me. There was something in Shelby's eyes when I asked her to watch over the little boy. *A twinkle? A glimmer of hope? Yeah, maybe something like that.* Whatever it was, it was nice to see. It reminded me of how she was when she was pregnant with Ryder. She loved everything about being pregnant and looked forward to the day that she would deliver our child and we would finally be a family. The minute I made her mine, we were already a family, and any children we had would just make our lives richer and stronger.

I shook my head and tried to get back to the reason why I came in here in the first place. Thinking about the past would only hurt my heart and jeopardize the progress we'd made.

"Hey, Tenley, it's Shane. I need a favor."

My call took longer than I thought it would, but Tenley would make some calls first thing in the morning for me and then would call me back. For now, she just told me to take care of the little boy and get a good night's rest. Yeah, good luck with that, but I promised I would try.

I made my way back to the living room and witnessed the sweetest sight. Shelby was holding the little boy in her arms and singing "You are my sunshine."

14

Doorstop miracle

Shelby

Shane still hadn't emerged from the office yet as I waited with the little boy, who was beginning to stir awake on our couch. He had light brown hair, kind of overgrown, but shaggy hair on little boys is adorable. I hadn't seen the color of his eyes yet, but I guessed they were brown. He was so small with his little hands tucked under his face.

When his eyes finally opened, he looked scared and quickly sat up on the couch, clutching the blanket to his chest.

"Hey, don't be frightened. You're safe here. My name is Shelby. Can you tell me your name?"

He moved his lips, but no words came out. I waited and then encouraged him to try again.

"It's okay, little one. You can tell me."

"Wyatt, my name is Wyatt."

"You see how easy that was? Now we're friends. Are you hungry? You must be, after that big nap. You know, on nights when it gets really cold and you can just feel the weather turning, I like to sit in front of the fire and drink a warm mug of hot chocolate."

"Me too," he said shyly.

"Wow! We have something in common. Okay, I just happen to have some right there in this thermos, but you can't drink hot chocolate without…"

"Marshmallows," he said excitedly.

It was clear this little boy had been through a lot. If something as simple as a mug of hot chocolate made him smile, I think I would give him just about anything he asked for.

"Yes! That would be perfect. Let me look here on my tray to see if I have some. You are in luck, Wyatt, because I happen to have marshmallows in two sizes. We have the mini size or the jumbo size that we can only fit about two in our mug, but if you choose the minis, we can fit a lot more. What do you say?"

"How about the mini kind?"

"Good choice, Wyatt, that's what I was going to choose." I poured the hot chocolate into our mugs, and then I slid over the bowl of marshmallows, which he dug in and took a big helping. My heart instantly melted and gushed over this little boy. I was right; his eyes were brown and big like saucers that probably could tell quite the story.

He took a timid sip from his mug and then seemed to go quiet on me. I asked if I could sit beside him, and he just nodded and gave me a half smile.

After I placed my own mug down, I began just humming, and then that humming turned into a song. I found myself singing "You are my sunshine," which I often did to relax. I hoped it would make him do the same. After I sang a few lines, he slowly eased his way closer to me to place his head down on my lap. My heart nearly burst watching him trust *me*—a stranger—take care of him. At first, I wasn't sure if I should do this, but he seemed as though he may have needed my comfort.

"You are my sunshine, my only sunshine. You make me happy when skies are gray. You'll never know, dear, how much I love you.

Please don't take my sunshine away." And with that, he was asleep again in my arms.

I found myself holding someone else's child when the only thing I wanted to do was hold my own. The emotions just took over, and the tears began to fall. When I looked up, I saw Shane standing in the doorway, watching me with a guarded smile on his face. *Did he know what I was thinking of at this moment? How could he not?* I wiped my face and shook off the sadness that always seemed to make its ugly return.

Shane knelt down in front of me and kissed me on my forehead, my nose, and my lips before telling me he loved me.

"I spoke to Tenley. She's going to make some calls in the morning for me and then will let me know what to do next. Shelby, is this okay? I mean, I never expected to find what I found out there. I mean, he's a little boy."

"I see that, Shane. He's in my arms, and I'm singing to him," I said, snapping at Shane.

"I'm sorry. I know this brings up a lot for you, and for us, but I didn't know what else to do. I could call my mom if you want me to."

"No. And confuse him more? His name is Wyatt. He didn't offer up his last name, but I didn't ask for one either. Shane, he's run away from something or someone, and I have this heavy feeling in my heart right now telling me that we have to help him. We have to do something for this little boy. I just don't know what that is."

"Well, I can think of one thing. He needs rest, and so do we. I'd put him in one of the spare bedrooms, but I'm afraid we will wake up in the morning and he won't be here."

"We have a rollaway bed that you could put in our room, and if he wakes up and is scared, we will be right beside him."

"Sounds like a plan, I'll be right back."

I handed off Wyatt to Shane, and he carried him upstairs to our bedroom. He shifted only once but quickly fell back asleep and slept soundly for the rest of the night.

I envied him because sleep was not to be found for me. I couldn't take my eyes off him. Every time he moved, I braced myself for what he would do, but it was my overactive imagination taking over.

"Baby, go to sleep. I have to go to work in two hours."

"Shane, we need to know where he came from. It's driving me insane to know that he was out there all by himself. My god, anything could have happened to him. This is a ranch, for crying out loud. He could have been mauled and killed by a wild animal or froze to death."

"Stop, stop right now, and shut your mind down and go to sleep. None of those things did happen, and I am eternally grateful for it. Right here and right now, we know his name is Wyatt and he's safe. Let's be thankful for that. Let's get a few hours of sleep, and then we will figure it out."

"Okay, I love you."

"I love you too. Now sleep."

He was right, he always was. I felt better with Shane's arms around me. I managed to sleep for a few hours, and then my eyes blinked open before the alarm sounded off. I shut it off and grabbed my robe before going downstairs to the smell of freshly brewed coffee. *Thank you, Shane.*

"Good morning, husband. How long have you been up?"

"Come on, babe. After you finally fell asleep, I maybe got another hour, and then I began my day doing all the morning chores before Luke and Wade made their way down to the barn. I'm taking the rest of the day off to…"

"Figure it out?" I asked.

"Exactly. That's what we are going to do, but not before I properly kiss you good morning."

Could this be possible? Can we keep him? I looked over my shoulder and watched my husband sip his coffee and just smile as if he already had a plan. Shane was always one to believe everything that was meant to work out would do exactly that. He and Jagger always said that Jamie was the philosophical one out of their group, but his wisdom and beliefs were within them too. It's crazy to entertain what is going through my head right now, *but what if this is our second chance? A miracle just placed in our lives? How can we argue with the universe when everything inside of me is screaming this is right?*

15

He's not ours, but can he be?

Shane

I didn't want to frighten him, so I sat at the end of the bed and waited for Wyatt to wake from his slumber. Last night when I found him, you could see the exhaustion lining his little face. God knows how long he was out in the elements until I found him in the cabin, and what scared me most was the fact that he did seek shelter but ran away because he was scared of my guys finding him. Where did he sleep that night when he couldn't return to the barn or cabin?

Shelby was downstairs finishing up a few things and patiently waited for me to bring him down so she could feed him with anything he asked for. I could tell she was happy; her eyes practically shone like diamonds this morning. Her dreams were probably filled with the possibility of keeping this boy and claiming him as our own. She didn't have to voice her thoughts to me. I just knew because I was thinking the same thing. *He must be orphaned. Why else would he be out here?*

While I was lost in my own thoughts, he finally stirred awake without me noticing. I heard him faintly say "Good morning," and then I was finally back to the present.

"Well, hello there. Good morning, Wyatt. How did you sleep?"

He slowly sat up against the headboard and rubbed the sleep out of his eyes. He let out a big yawn and then smiled, which made my heart full of want.

"Good morning…" He stopped.

"It's Shane. My name is Shane."

"Shane," he said a couple of times and then said, "Hi Shane."

I just smiled and let out a small laugh. "Are you hungry? You must be, after sleeping so many hours. Can you come downstairs with me and have some breakfast?"

He looked unsure and then twisted his small hands in the blankets. "Just breakfast?"

What was he afraid of? I thought and then simply said, "Yeah, just breakfast. Come on, the pancakes await."

He practically leaped out from under the covers and into my arms. He placed his head on my shoulder, and I just let him do it. This boy was in desperate need of being cared for. After we finish with breakfast, I will call our family doctor to have a look at him to make sure he's really okay.

With Wyatt still in my arms, we entered the kitchen to find Shelby looking worried, standing between my father, Brock, and Ren Parrish, accompanied by Sheriff Sam Tillerson. I held the boy closer to my chest, and my father gave me a worrisome look.

There was no way I was going to have a scene here in the middle of my kitchen with a frightened boy to witness. I handed off Wyatt to Shelby and asked her to fix Wyatt a plate of breakfast while I talked to our visitors in my office. She extended her arms out in front of Wyatt, and he easily went from my arms to Shelby's, smiling the entire time. My eyes found hers as she held him. My god, he weighed next to nothing and was so small in my wife's arms. I nodded with a look of understanding, and Shelby turned to tend to Wyatt.

"Good morning," I said and then invited all of them to follow me out and down the hall where we could speak in private. Once they were in and seated, I closed the heavy door and took a seat at my desk. "So, what do I owe the pleasure of an early morning visit from all of you?" I questioned.

"Shane, I think it's pretty clear as to why we're here," Tillerson said. "Two weeks ago, a young boy vanished from a town tour that included a trip to the museum and finished up with horseback riding. It had been planned and arranged by Cathedral Home for Children. The boy you were holding in your arms matches the description of the missing child that was last seen right here on The Fairchild Ranch."

I sat there completely stunned and then looked over to my father, Brock, and Ren, who all had their faces down and looked almost embarrassed that this could happen here on our ranch.

"Sheriff, allow me to explain."

"Oh, please do, Shane. I can't wait to hear it."

"Watch the attitude, Sam," my father reprimanded Tillerson, who was also a friend but certainly not acting like one right now.

I put my hands up to calm everyone down. "Okay, let me begin by saying that I was not even aware that we had a booking like that. In recent months, I have pulled back from the day-to-day tasks over at the dude ranch, and that includes the tour bookings. I only recently became proactive again, and for the last week or so, I was busy getting the cabins ready. Luke and Wade had alerted me that one of the cabins had been disturbed, and items from the cabin, along with some stock, was missing from the barn. I didn't really believe it was a big deal, but then my curiosity got the better of me, and the need to solve the mystery intensified. I am in charge of all Fairchild operations, and I had to take it seriously."

"How so?"

"I set up night cameras down by the cabins that would pick up anything that came into view. After waiting several hours, I was about to go home, and then there it was. A small image appeared. I thought it might be a coyote or even a wolf. We've had them before threatening the livestock, but since that's not an issue on the fairground side, I investigated. It ran from me, and I had my gun ready for anything. Once

I cornered it to the bushes that ran along the back, I was completely taken by surprise to discover that it was a little boy and not a wild animal."

"Dad, Brock, Ren," I addressed them and not Tillerson. "He was scared, so scared. It was late into the night, and I didn't know what else to do but bring him home, feed him, and then after a good night's rest, which he clearly needed, I was going to deal with this in the morning, but you beat me to it. I did call Tenley, and she said she would make some calls."

Tillerson then addressed me. "I got a call from the state trooper's office after they received a call from Tenley. I guess whatever she told them was enough to run this lead, and here I am. He's going to have to come with me."

"No! You can't do that," said Shelby, who just walked in on our conversation.

I rose from my seat and walked around the desk. "Shelby, calm down. We are going to figure this out. Where's Wyatt?" I kept my voice low and steady to do my best to reassure my wife. I knew she was frightened after hearing what Sam said. It was clear she'd already made her mind up about the little boy.

"He's upstairs with your mom. She brought over clothes and is giving him a bath. Please, Sheriff Tillerson, let him stay with us, at least until you work it out with his group home. We have everything he needs here. Why send him back to a large facility that probably has too many children to care for when you have two willing foster parents right here that can tend to his care? Look around the room, Sheriff. We are a big family, and we can take care of him."

Knowing what we'd been through, Sam looked sad for Shelby, but he had a job to do first, no matter how much he wanted to help us. No one could resist Shelby and those blue eyes that burned right into your soul. She would block the door if she had to before allowing Wyatt to leave with Sam. He let out a sigh and then said to give him some time while he made a few phone calls. She was satisfied with his answer and then wrapped her arms around my neck and smiled.

My father raised an eyebrow at me, probably trying to figure out what was going through my mind at the moment. *If he asked me, I don't think I could really say, because one part of me just wants to care and protect that little boy from everything and everyone who has ever hurt him. The other is not to hurt my wife. We are both on solid ground again and continuing to work on our marriage, but any little shake-up can set us back again, and there is a part of me that doesn't want to risk that.* I just looked at my father and gave him my best encouraging look. Not sure if he believed it, but it was all I could do.

Ren already made his exit while Brock stayed behind to talk to me for a minute. "Son, this is not your fault. We all take accountability on why this boy was here on the ranch. Although this ranch carries my name, we all own a part of it and will share the responsibility and consequences. I know I speak for all of us that we are happy our little wanderer is safe. Keep me posted, and I'll check in with you later. I need to take care of a few things, but please keep your temper in check with Sam. He's not the enemy."

"Thank you, Brock."

He patted my shoulder and gave it a squeeze and then joined Ren and gestured for my dad to follow. "Kip, we have that meeting in town, remember?"

"Yeah, I'm coming." He reached for his hat and then turned back to me. "I'll talk to you later?"

"Yeah, later." It was all I could say and then looked at Shelby, who looked as if she reached her limit of patience. I closed the door after them and took a breath before talking with my wife.

"Baby, listen to me, okay? You need to slow down a bit and pump the breaks here. I saw your face when you walked in, and I can guess what you're thinking."

"Oh please, Shane, I'm not crazy here. You mean to tell me that you're not thinking the same thing? Did you ever think that maybe this is the universe telling us something? A cosmic sign?"

"Maybe, I don't know."

"No, you do know. This is what you and Jagger believe. Hell, everyone believes in the sun, moon, and the stars around here. You all have your own personal angel up there doing your bidding here on earth, and when I finally believe in it too, you doubt it."

"That's not true. Please, babe, you need to listen to me. We don't know this kid, and we certainly don't know his situation or what led him to run away and hide out here. Shelby, it's been two weeks that this little boy has been out there all alone. We need to find out more before we do anything else."

"You want him, Shane. I can see it in your eyes. Just tell me what you are thinking right now, and then I'll let the subject drop."

"Okay, yes, I thought of keeping him. Is that what you want to hear? That I allowed my mind to entertain the possibility of becoming this boy's father?"

"Yes, and thank you for telling me the truth. Just do me a favor and believe in what's possible for today, and then tomorrow we can go back to figuring it out. I have this feeling that fate has stepped in and dropped our…what? Third or maybe fourth chance at parenthood?"

I didn't have the opportunity to respond, with my mom walking down the stairs with Wyatt. He cleaned up pretty good. Mama had dressed him in jeans and a hooded sweatshirt, along with a new pair of sneakers that had the flashing soles on the bottom. *My mom is a wonder. It's like she knows what to do when the rest of us are just still figuring it out.*

"Hey, mama, thanks for taking care of Wyatt while we talked things out."

"My pleasure, son. He's a doll." She ran her fingers through his overgrown hair, and I'm sure her mama bear instincts were already sounding off that he needed a long overdue haircut. She smiled and winked at me, and then I nearly busted out in laughter. "I'm going to catch up with your daddy and then do some office stuff with Connie, unless you need me here."

"No, we will be fine."

"You know, if you change your mind, I'll be right back down."

"I know, mama, and thank you for all your help this morning." I kissed her on her cheek and then practically shoved her out the door. I knew that if I said I needed her, then she would have never left, and I already had my hands full with Shelby.

"Okay, how about we three go inside to the living room and have a talk?" I reached for Wyatt's hand, and he took it with no hesitation. Shelby was apprehensive, but she didn't need to be.

"Wyatt, why did you run away? Can you tell me about it?"

"Shane…" Shelby cut in, but I raised my hand up.

"Honey, it's going to be okay."

"Wyatt, it's okay. Do you remember what I told you last night about being safe here?"

He nodded.

"Good, so you can talk to me. Why did you run?" I asked.

"I hate that place. The other kids push me around, and no one ever does anything about it."

"Do they hurt you? The other kids?"

"Once. A big kid punched me in my stomach and took the candy bar that Mrs. Rosie gave to me."

"Who's Mrs. Rosie? Does she work there?"

"She helps out a couple of times a week and is nice to me."

"She gives you candy?"

"Yes, and hugs too, but if the other kids see, then they tease me and call me a baby."

"Well, where I come from, hugs are awesome, and I never turn away a big, old bear hug."

"What's a bear hug?"

"You never heard of a bear hug?"

"Nope."

"Okay, let me show you. Ms. Shelby, care to help me out here?"

"I would love to." She laughed.

I stood up and wrapped my arms around Shelby, easily lifting her off the floor. She giggled in my chest, and then I twirled her around the living room just for the extra love I knew she was enjoying.

Wyatt was smiling and then asked if he could have one too. Shelby asked if she could give him one, and he smiled brightly and stretched his arms out to her.

I nearly cried at the sight of the two of them. God, she was so beautiful, especially when she was happy. I had forgotten how long it had been since I'd seen my wife this way. Yes, we'd been better, but today she was taking my breath away as I watched her swing Wyatt around the room and listened to the sweet sounds of them laughing.

I quietly excused myself from the room when I noticed Tillerson standing in the doorway. There was no way I was going to stop my wife and Wyatt from their moment of happiness, knowing it might be short-lived depending on what Sam told me.

"Hey, what did you find out?" I inquired.

"Your girl Tenley definitely kicked the hornet's nest down in Laramie."

"Yes, she can be very persuasive when she wants something. What do we know, Sam?"

"He's technically a ward of the state who has been in foster care for over two years since his mother waived her parental rights to him. He's been moved around a lot and always ends up back at Cathedral."

"Why is that? Should I be concerned?"

"I don't think so. It's more logistics. The past fosters were just temporary, and most of them had too many kids under their small roof. This kid just happened to be at the bottom and got kicked back a lot."

"What about the biological father?"

"The father listed on the birth certificate was killed on active duty while in Iraq just three years ago. The mother, Caitlyn Jacoby, totally went off the rails from there and got into some trouble with a couple of DUI's along with several arrests involving multiple counts of possession, etc. Shane, it's a long and complicated record, and it all seems to have happened after her boyfriend and father of Wyatt died. She's been in and out of rehab trying to get back on her feet but taking care of her son was not in the cards, and she didn't have any family to claim him, so she handed him off to the state."

"Fucking A, Sam! He's seven years old, for cripes sake. How the hell did he make it on this ranch for two fucking weeks without one fucking person knowing he was here?"

"Shane, will you calm down before you have a stroke? The good part in all of this is you found him last night, and he's not alone now. Look, I didn't mean to be insensitive earlier. I know what you and Shelby have gone through, and I'm not blind to see that you don't want to let this boy go."

"Yeah, man, I really need to work on my poker face a little bit better. I thought I was better at hiding my feelings."

"That may be true, but when you have Shelby acting the same way you are, I think it's obvious and plain as day to the rest of us. So, this is what that tenacious lawyer did for you. She was able to grant you temporary custody of Wyatt until the courts can get a hearing on the books. A caseworker will be coming out later today or tomorrow the latest, and then the real work begins."

"Which is what?" I asked perplexed.

"The road to adoption, if that's what you want."

"Holy shit, my head is spinning right now. I have to talk to Shelby."

"Yes, my answer is yes!" I heard her call out from the doorway. "Yes, we want him!"

Oh, fuck! Was she listening the whole time? Of course she wants him, and a part of me wants the same, but again, the fucking fear that was still in me was always present when it came to my wife and our marriage. She seemed stronger, but are we both ready for this?

I looked back to Shelby, who was nodding her answer and telling me with her eyes that everything was going to be okay.

16

We can do this

Shelby

I knew it was crazy, Shane did too, but I just didn't care when everything inside of me was screaming that this was right for us. Wyatt coming into our lives at this very moment was meant to be.

Shane looked like a deer caught in the headlights after I interrupted his conversation with Sam, but after hearing Shane explode, I knew it was time to make my presence known. Very few people had the power to calm my man down, and I knew he was ready to lose his control after he heard Wyatt's story. This little boy was literally just left in the hands of strangers and had to endure bullying and basic care for his well-being, if you want to call it that.

Shane was called away on ranch business and hadn't returned yet, leaving me with Wyatt. After he ate breakfast, he helped me clean up and load the dishwasher, all with a smile on his face. Here was this little person in my huge kitchen helping me with something as simple as dishes. He looked comfortable and so much better than he did from last night.

Kip returned and wanted to check in with us. I assured him I was fine, but my father-in-law wanted to talk, so Wyatt went down to the barn with Kathleen to look at the horses, and I was here, readying myself for a lecture.

"How you doing, darling?" True to form, he always made that his first question.

"I'm fine. Really, you don't have to worry about me."

"Yeah, try again. Come on, you know you can talk to me."

I let out a sigh and tried not to roll my eyes, but Kip was very intuned to his family and was not letting this go.

"I want to keep him. I can't explain it, I just have this strong feeling that having this little boy come into our lives is a good thing." I wiped away my tears knowing I could not hold back my feelings from him. "This is right. I know it is," I said again, and then I just cried and let it all out.

He didn't say anything but pulled me into his strong arms and let me have my moment. I never had this connection with my father, and the minute I met Kip Rhodes, it was like I knew him forever with the unconditional love he always showed for me.

"Shelby, look at me." I did once he released me. He handed me a tissue box, and I composed myself enough to hear him out. "I wasn't going to try to talk you out of this. You need to know that from the start, but it also doesn't mean that I'm not worried for you, and for my son. I need you to slow down for a second and just take a breath. It's obvious that little boy needs care. It's clear to anyone who meets him that he's been neglected and certainly not cared for like a child should be. Group homes are overloaded with hundreds of Wyatt's in the same situation, maybe even in worse conditions. This boy is beyond lucky to have chosen the right time and place to make a run for it and find you and Shane. It's as if he chose you two to save him."

"Yes, you get it. I knew you would."

"Yes, having said that, I'm going to say one more thing that you may not like, but it has to be said."

"Go for it, I'm ready."

"He won't replace the son you lost. You know that, right?"

"Kip, I do know that. How could you say those words to me? Our baby boy will always have a special place in our heart, and we know he's irreplaceable, but that doesn't mean there's no room for anyone else. Adoption was never off the table for us, and now Wyatt is here. A gift, a sign from the universe, the angels, I don't care what you call it. We have a chance here, Kip, and I know we can be good and loving parents to this little boy. I know we can. Please believe me. I'm not trying to erase the past; I'm just trying to live in the now and find the happiness for our future."

"Okay, that's good enough for me. I had to ask. I'm sorry."

"It's fine. I know you love us and want the best for us. It's going to work out, you'll see." And with that, he hugged me, and we were okay.

"I have to go, sweetheart. Shane should be coming back soon, and you two need to talk."

"Okay, I'll see you out." I waved him off as Tenley was parking her truck. The front door was revolving today with visitors, but she was one guest I welcomed with open arms, because she would be the one to help us keep Wyatt.

"Hey, where's Jamie? You didn't bring him with you?" I asked, looking over her shoulder.

"No, not this time. He's with Jagger having some daddy time. And as much as I love my son, he would be a distraction when I need to focus on you. Where's Shane?"

"He should be back soon. Some cattle broke down the fence line, and he was gathering them back in."

"That's fine. We can start without him and then catch him up to speed. So, here's the file on Wyatt Adam Jacoby. He was born on February 20th, just had a birthday, which makes him seven. As you know, his father was killed overseas, and mom is gone to parts unknown. With all rights relinquished for her child, she can just come and go as she pleases. Her last known address was Tulsa, Oklahoma, with no forwarding we know about. It was a sober house, I think. I have to look into it, but it's what I have so far."

Tenley was like the Energizer Bunny on crack. She was talking a mile a minute, and all I heard was February 20th. Anything after that was just a garbled mess, like the teacher in Charlie Brown. My stomach tightened, and I went silent. When she finally caught on to what was happening to me, she called out my name.

"Shelby, what's going on?" she asked with concern.

I held my head in my hands and tried very hard not to go back there to that day when time just stood still. I was having a hard time catching my breath. I wasn't immune to a panic attack and suffered from a few of them after I lost our son. Tenley handed me a glass of water and instructed me to take small sips and to breathe. She spoke softly as my body slowly recovered from the surge of adrenaline.

"Shelby, talk to me," she said a little louder and squatted down in front of me.

"I'm sorry. I'm okay. Tenley…the date."

"Date? What date? I'm confused."

"His birthday is the same day as…" I almost couldn't say the words, and then realization was written all over Tenley's face and she knew.

"Oh, my goodness, I am so stupid. I didn't even put two and two together. When I'm in lawyer mode, it's all I see. I didn't mean to be insensitive."

"No, don't be silly, you're not. I just kind of shut down for a second after I heard the date. You know to everyone else it's just a day on the calendar, but to us, it's life-changing. Tenley, I have no doubt whatsoever that this is a sign. A miracle we've been praying for."

"I'm not following."

"Tenley, don't you see? Wyatt was born on February 20th. My accident was on February 20th. While our son died, another life came into the world, and now that same life is here. He's here in our life and our home, needing a family."

"Oh, Shelby, I want to believe everything you just said, and I promise you that I will do everything in my power to make this happen for you and Shane, but it's a lot of legal issues to navigate through. Everything you need to begin this process, I have here for you in this file. Let me just go over a few things with you, and then I will answer any questions you may have. Sound good?"

"Sure, please, go on."

"First off, we need to fill out your application to become a certified foster parent. Approval usually takes three to six months, but I may be able to have the state grant a petition for emergency custody because of the circumstances involving Wyatt running away and the reasons behind that. It's a 50/50 shot, but I say let's go for it. Secondly, you should prepare yourselves for spending another nine to eighteen months to complete the inquiry, orientation, and preparation classes, which will include home study visits."

"Okay, hang in there, Shelby. I'm almost through with the hard parts. The process has already begun with the state and he's already been assigned a new caseworker of my choosing. You will like her, she's amazing. Look, it's abundantly clear that someone has dropped the ball with this boy. It's also incredibly embarrassing for the state to have a child under their care and then he suddenly vanishes. For whatever reason, they tried to keep this quiet. I smell a cover-up and once I get to the bottom of it all, heads are going to roll with the major ass-kicking I'm going to deliver."

"His disappearance should have been national news, but it wasn't, which explains why a lot of locals didn't even know about it. It's murky waters and a hell of a lot of red tape, but again, not impossible. I am a very good lawyer, and I will be representing you, so you're already winning."

"Lastly, as I mentioned, we have a new caseworker. Her name is Roberta Davidson. While I was down at the department of child services, I ran into her and told her about Wyatt. I didn't even have the chance to submit a request for a new point of contact. Roberta volunteered and is an excellent person to have on our side. She will be a key player in the process, appointed to ensure that the child's needs and rights to safety and well-being are met."

"Roberta will communicate with you until the adoption is finalized. So, that's pretty much it. Do you have any questions?"

"Tenley, I'm not sure you even paused between all you have said to take a breath. I can't imagine doing your job, but you seem to do it very well, which makes what I say next be hard to hear, but it needs to be said."

"Have I overstepped here? I thought you wanted my help?" She looked confused.

"I do, we do, but is there another way we can expedite this nine to eighteen-month process?"

I watched Tenley place all the paperwork down and put her shoulders back in a defiant stance. "Before another word is spoken here, we need to be clear and on the same page, and from what you just said, it does not coincide with my plan of action regarding you and Shane adopting Wyatt."

"Tenley, just take your lawyer hat off just for a second and just be a mom. What kind of person abandons their own child and just leaves them hanging out in the wind for strangers to care for him? He's scared. By the looks of him, his care has been neglected. He may be seven years old, but he looks the size of age four, and don't even get me started on his weight. He's skin and bones. Look where we live, Tenley. Your father, your husband, my husband, and their fathers own the biggest ranch in Wyoming, and one of the largest in the country. Surely, we can use that to influence a few bureaucrats to see things our way? We have money, and with money comes power. Those two things make the world go around. We can move this process along, can't we, Tenley? There has to be someone we can call upon to help us."

"Wow! I think I might need a drink or two. Shelby, this is not how it works. There's rules, many steps, and a lot of time in between. I know the process can be grueling and beyond stressful, but it's not impossible to obtain."

"No, you don't know the process and probably never will! And why should you? When you're still able to have children!" I shouted and immediately regretted my words. I inhaled deeply and then released my breath. "I'm sorry, Tenley. I didn't mean it."

"Yeah, you did, and I'm not going to sit here and tell you that I know how you feel and have been where you are, because I haven't. We mourned your loss with you, and although it didn't happen to me, doesn't mean I didn't feel your pain. There are not enough apologies in the universe to say to you and Shane, but we tried because we love you. I'm here today as your friend and a lawyer, because I know I can help you. Believe me, I want to, but for you to ask what you just asked me is crossing the boundary of friendship and most importantly the law."

"Everything you just said is absolutely correct, but I'm desperate here and will do anything I have to do to keep this boy. He can't go back into the system and to that place. He just can't. Please help us. I know you have connections, important ones that you can call in a favor. I know all about your life in New York City. Shane told me. Please, Tenley, help me become a mom. You can do this for me, and more importantly, you owe Shane."

The cold dagger of a look that Tenley aimed toward me had the power to literally make me weak in the knees, but I was out of options and would do anything I had to do to keep Wyatt with us.

I knew shoving old history from her past was not the smartest way to make Tenley help me, and I also knew if Shane found out about this, he would be disappointed and hurt by my actions. It was his past as well, and he put it behind him a long time ago.

I waited and prepared myself for the fallout from my words, but it never came. She stood emotionless and simply said, "I have to go. I'll leave this file with you so you and Shane can read it over, and then I will be in touch." She turned away and began walking out.

"Tenley, please!" I reached for her arm to stop her from leaving.

She jerked it back as if I had burned her. *Didn't I?* "Tenley, I know what I'm asking of you."

"Really? Because it sounds more like demanding. Who the hell do you think you are? And where do you get off reminding me of a time in my life that has absolutely nothing to do with you? Just because you are Shane's wife doesn't mean you get a free pass to give an opinion pertaining to me or my history with him. Do not believe for one second that you understand any part of that time, because you can never, unless you were there living it with us, and you weren't. Shelby, no matter how much we move forward in our lives, the past is always there on some level. I know it and have made peace with it. What I didn't know was that a person I have come to care about and welcome into our family would use it to get what she wants and not give a damn on who she hurts."

"I'm sorry, Tenley. I didn't mean it the way it came out."

"Save it, because lying will not help you. It's just eye-opening to me knowing how you really see me. I thought we were friends."

"We are, the best of friends."

"You can keep telling yourself that and maybe you will believe it, but no friend I have would ever do what you just did. You make me sound like some boss bitch that just snaps her fingers and greases the right hands to get what I want. To be frank, you know nothing about my career, and the things you think you know have been overdramatized to tell a good story. Stick to what you know, and I'll do the same."

She was already pissed off at me, so why stop now? "Says the officer of the court who singlehandedly brought down two major crime lords of one of the biggest mob families in New York. You're going to stand there in all your righteousness and tell me that you always played by the rules, always followed a strict code of ethics? Because if you say yes, then I know you will be lying. I will risk bending the law if it means allowing Shane and me to keep this boy and make him our son. I will risk you being angry with me. I will risk losing your friendship.

I'll do anything for Wyatt. Please, Tenley, I need you to do this. If not for me, do it for Shane. He already loves that little boy."

"You have him for the next few days, at least until we are granted a hearing. It all depends on when the judge is available to hear our case. I'll be in touch. I have to go."

She didn't break, not for a second. She had nerves of steel, and you never knew what she was thinking behind that tough persona of hers, especially when she was wearing her lawyer hat. Even when I reminded her of something so hurtful from her long friendship with Shane, she still mentally kicked my ass, leaving me to wonder if once she gets home, she will change her mind altogether on helping us. I stood there in silence as I watched Tenley speed away in her truck, leaving me not knowing where to go from here.

I knew Shane would be angry with me, but I had to try, and I would take full responsibility for it. It wouldn't be the last mistake I made, and I'd been notorious for grave errors of judgment, but not this time. This was right. Someone had to fight for Wyatt, and it might as well be me.

I wasn't going to stress over it any longer. I grabbed my coat and made my way to the barn to see the reason for my smile. He looked so happy petting Yankee and the rest of the horses. This ranch was magical, especially for children.

"Hey, Wyatt, would you like to give Yankee a carrot?"

"Yes, please," he said excitedly. Kathleen left us on our own, and it was just us in this big barn surrounded by horses. "Will he bite me?" he asked curiously.

"Not if you do it right. You see, Yankee belongs to Shane. He's very loyal to his rider, but that doesn't mean he won't be friends with you. He's a Paint Horse. Do you know what that is?"

"No, ma'am."

"Well, he's a quarter horse, but what makes him special is his coloring. He's brown and white, when other quarter horses are just brown. Shane wanted different, and he raised Yankee up from a colt. He's very strong and beautiful too. He also loves compliments. Right, Yankee?" He picked the right time to nudge my shoulder, and then I knew he was giving me the okay for Wyatt to feed him.

"Okay, Yankee is being so welcoming today. How about we give him a juicy apple instead?"

"Yeah, that's better."

"I agree, so hold out your hand palm up and slowly move it close to Yankee. Don't be afraid. I'm right here with you." He slowly followed my instructions and then laughed when Yankee took the apple from him.

"That was perfect. Okay, always stay on the horse's side." I instructed and watched Wyatt do exactly what I told him. "There you go. Now gently pet the side of his neck in smooth strokes." He was standing on the block, and his little hand got lost in Yankee's coat as he moved his hand up and down his long neck. "There now, how was that?" I asked and then gave Yankee another apple.

"Everything. I never did that before. You don't see many horses where I live."

"I'm sure you don't, but around here, that's all there is."

"Thank you for letting me feed him."

"You're welcome, buddy. How about we go back up to the house and make some cookies? Would you like to help me with that?"

"Yes! Chocolate chip?" he said excitedly.

"Is there any other kind? Chocolate chip is my favorite to make."

"I never made cookies, but I know how to eat them. Mrs. Rosie used to bring them to the home for us but always gave me extra."

"Sounds like Mrs. Rosie is a really nice lady. Maybe one day I'll get to meet her."

He just smiled and said nothing more. I said goodbye to Yankee and then held Wyatt's hand as we walked back to the house in silence. I wanted to ask him questions about the group home and Mrs. Rosie, but I couldn't push him. So, baking was the next best thing to do.

17

Is this right for us?

Shane

"Thanks, man, for helping me out here today. I think with those new stabilizers on the fence posts, we shouldn't have any more cattle coming through. Shane! Earth to Shane! Are you listening to me?"

"What?" I said in a much louder voice then I intended to.

"Hey, take it easy. I was just thanking you for the help, but clearly, you didn't hear me."

"I'm sorry, Jagger. It's not you. I just can't forget what you told me and then to have Tenley confirm it. What in the hell was she thinking? I swear, my head was spinning the entire drive back to the ranch."

"Did you talk to Shelby about it?"

"No, I didn't know how to bring it up to her. The minute I saw her face, I knew it wasn't the right time. She never stops smiling. It's only been a few days, and it's like Shelby has just flipped a switch and has completely moved Wyatt in and already is way too attached. Jagger, we haven't even heard from a case worker yet, and who knows when we will go to court. The longer Wyatt remains with us, the harder it's going to be to let him go if they take him from us."

He placed his hammer down into the toolbox and put the bed of my truck down. He hopped on and reached for a beer out of the cooler. "Drink this and take a breath. I'll admit my girl was a little taken back with what Shelby asked of her, but she doesn't spook easily, you know that. Tenley is amazing at what she does and will do her very best, but no one can ask her to break the law."

"More like bending, and she's done it before."

"First off, we don't speak of before, and you damn well know why that is, so shut the fuck up about it. I can't believe you think those two situations are the same. Tenley is not the same person she was back in New York. It's almost another life."

"Look, I'm sorry. I don't want to fight, especially with you. I'm just at a crossroads right now, and I'm not sure what road to take that will make everyone in my life happy."

"You know, a very smart person told me a story about crossroads and how they affect your life. It's like a four-way intersection, each arrow facing a new way. You're standing in the middle of it, not know-ing what to do. And then…it hits you. This overwhelming jolt to your system that is so deep inside that you just know which road to take. Once you're on it, you know it's the right path that you'll get the an-swers to your questions, and it will be alright. All roads lead home, Shane."

"Fucking Jamie, it never fails." We both clinked our beer bottles together.

"Yeah, he's laughing right about now, but he was right when he gave me that advice. And now since he's not here to give it to you, the honor is bestowed on me. You need to go home and talk with Shelby. Figure it out together."

"What if we can't? What if she already loves this boy so much that she's willing to sacrifice anything and everyone to keep him?"

"I guess you won't know until you talk with her. Go home."

"Hey, guys, I hate to break up this testosterone moment, but I just received a call from the clerk down in Judge Clayton's office. Your hearing is on Monday morning's docket, first thing."

"Tenley, we haven't even talked with a social worker. How can this be happening already?"

"You don't need to. You've been vetted by the state, and all your paperwork is submitted, granting temporary custody to you and Shelby. What happens on Monday is that you will present yourselves in front of the judge and tell him why you want to become parents to Wyatt. How you will promise to love him and always care for him and his needs. After that, you will most likely have a home visit or two and then more paperwork, ending with the adoption day. Again, the judge will make you swear under oath and hold you to your promises for Wyatt, and once that is done, he will sign off on it and make it a matter of public record that you, Shane Rhodes, are now a father. You go home and be happy for the rest of your lives."

If I wasn't sitting on the bed of my truck, I might have fallen over. Jagger was in awe of his wife, and frankly, so was I.

"Tenley, I don't know what to say right now."

She raised her hands up, and because I knew her so well, she was doing everything in her power to hold back her emotions.

"Don't say anything. Just be a great dad to that precious little boy, because he needs you and you need him." She hugged me and then placed a kiss on my cheek before turning and walking back into the house. I thought I might have seen her wipe a tear away from her face, but she would never let me see that.

Jagger clapped a hand on my shoulder, and we knew we didn't need to say anything more to each other. The unspoken truth weighed heavily between us that you could have sliced it with a knife.

"Daddy, daddy, come play with me." We heard next and then looked up to see Tenley holding their eighteen-month-old son, Jamie. Man, he was so cute and the spitting image of Jagger. He nearly sprinted toward his son and took him from Tenley, who just half smiled at me before closing their front door, leaving me out here alone.

A part of me wanted to knock on their door and beg Tenley to talk to me. She didn't have to say the words. I knew what she did for us, and I also knew what it cost her. *Is it right for me to just let her compromise her values in what she believes to be wrong? Especially when it comes to her career? Fuck! I can't let her do that.*

I jumped off my truck and was going to knock on their door when my phone buzzed in my pocket with a text message. It was from Jagger. *What was he doing? Watching me from the window? Damn, he knew me too well. I hate when he's right. I'm overthinking this amazing gift I've been given.*

JAGGER: *Go the fuck home! You're freaking my wife out, and I promised her many orgasms tonight, which won't happen until you go the fuck home!*

ME: *Okay, I'm going, and did I really need to hear about your sex life?*

JAGGER: *Fuck yeah, you did! Now go home and give some to your wife. Bye!*

I pocketed my phone and just shoved the rest of the bullshit aside and went home to my wife.

"Hey, you're a little late tonight. We were starving and went ahead with dinner, but I saved you a plate. It won't take me but a minute to warm up."

"Babe, dinner can wait, but what I have to tell you cannot. Where's Wyatt?"

"He's inside with your mom and dad."

"Shit! Tonight was dinner with the family, and I totally spaced."

"It's fine. I fed your father two helpings of pie."

"That works. Let me just send him a text to watch Wyatt, while we take a ride to talk."

"It's that bad that you can't tell me here?"

"It's not bad at all. Come on, babe, let's take a ride. It's too cold for the horses, so the truck will have to do." She placed her hand on mine as I led her around to the other side. Mom waved from the porch. She knew what I was doing. I wasn't ready to talk to anyone but my wife, and I needed to clear my head before seeing Wyatt again.

I drove us down to the river and parked my truck. It was a full moon tonight, so it was like the lights had been turned on out here. She held her hands in her lap and twisted her fingers, something she always tended to do when she was nervous. I reached for them and held them in mine to calm her.

"Babe, listen to me, please. I was working with Jagger today, as you know, and I finished up with the fences down at his place. While I was there, I talked with Tenley, and she gave me some news about Wyatt and the upcoming hearing."

"We have a hearing?" She sounded surprised.

"We sure do, and it's on Monday morning."

"But? Other than the initial submittals, we haven't really talked to anyone beyond the first phase. What happened to eighteen months?"

It was time to confront her with what I know. "Seriously? Are you going to sit there and pretend you don't know what I am talking about here? Come on, babe, don't play around, especially with me." She sat there in silence for a few minutes, and then when I believed she would at least look remorseful for what she did, she straightened her shoulders and came clean.

"Yes, I inadvertently asked Tenley to work outside the lines for us, and it looks like she did. Despite our argument, she did this for Wyatt, because she knows he deserves a chance at having a family who will love and take care of him."

"Oh my god, I can't fucking believe this. Shelby, do you realize what you have done here?"

"Yes, I do, and I'm not the least bit sorry for it. It has brought us one step closer to becoming parents. Do you want me to feel bad over this? Because if that's what you are waiting for, then I'm sorry, Shane, but I will not do that. Have you read the statistics on how many foster children are in our state alone? How many children have been waiting to be adopted? The numbers are staggering. What about the leeches that just do it for a paycheck at the end of the month? Because, Shane, they're out there and do unscrupulous things all in the name of money and greed, and they don't put the children they foster first. I know you're angry, but please, if I'm guilty of anything, it's wanting and loving Wyatt so much that I lost my head. After the way Tenley left, I didn't believe she would help us at all, and now you're telling me that she practically handed us a miracle on a silver platter."

"You should have told me. I hated hearing it from Tenley."

"So what? She ran from here and did not rest until she told you what I did? Dammit! I hate this. I'm not that insecure woman I was when I first met her, and now I feel as if I am right back there on the day we met."

"God!" I shouted loud enough to wake the dead. "You still don't get it? My past will forever be entwined with Jagger, Tenley, and Jamie. I made my share of mistakes—we all did—but we also made peace with them a very long time ago. So, to hear that you undermined my friendship with them—for what, to get a point across?—just hurts me. It wasn't Tenley that first told me what you practically demanded her to do, it was Jagger. He felt I had a right to know what happened between our wives. When she arrived home, she was visibly upset. They don't keep secrets from one another. It was only after I heard the story that I went to Tenley, and she confirmed what Jagger said to be true. So, she didn't run and tattle on you. Please, would it kill you to think just a little better of her?"

"I'm sorry, Shane. I'm so sorry. I will never do anything like that again. You believe me, right?" she said, holding back the tears I knew would fall.

"Yes, I believe and forgive you. Now kiss me," I said. I followed with, "Shelby, you are amazing and are the woman that I love most in this world. My life really didn't begin until I met you. Tenley is like a sister to me and is married to my best friend. I swear you have nothing to ever worry about. Yes, I'm protective of Tenley. I've known her since she came into the world, but that's where it stops. I just feel that although your intentions were good, you went about it the wrong way and used *our* friend to get what you want, and that's what I'm angry about. You kept this from me, and it hurts because we promised to be better than that."

"I'm sorry. I'm sorry. Please don't give up on me."

"Stop with the apologies. It's over now."

She slowly calmed and kissed me again. "Shane, I know I am a work in progress and drive you absolutely insane, but it comes from a good place."

"It does, and you never have to worry about me leaving. If you want the truth, it's me that is always worrying about you leaving me. For a long time after Ryder's death, I slept with one eye open, fearing that you would be gone in the morning. You were angry with me for so long, I didn't think we would ever get back what we had, and now here we are getting ready to adopt this amazingly smart little boy whose eyes light up with just feeding my horse an apple. All I see is purity in his eyes, and all he wants in return is to be loved and cared for. I love you so much. I've been watching you with him, and I just stand back in the quiet, barely able to hold back my tears. Seriously, Shelby, you take my breath away. You were meant to be a mother, and you were right."

"About?"

"I swear you always make me say it."

"It helps."

"I believe in us and our family, and Wyatt coming into our lives was a direct message from the angels above. It has to be, because I can't think of any other reason why he was put in our path."

"Oh, I love you, Shane," she cried out as she lunged herself into my arms. "Thank you, baby."

"Thank you, Shelby. Thank you for believing in our family during the times I doubted. It's going to be okay. We've come too far for it not to. Let's go home to our son."

18

Plus one

Shelby

"*Let's go home to our son.*" When Shane said those words to me, I knew without a doubt that no matter what happened from tonight on, he believed in us and our family. I nearly cried happy tears all the way home. I was so unbelievably happy that I could not contain my joy and excitement.

Shane held my hand and focused on the road while I just beamed with joy and hope for our future. When we went inside, Kathleen put a finger to her lips to quiet us. Wyatt had fallen asleep in Kip's arms while he read him a story. We had been gone longer than expected, and she told us that he couldn't keep his eyes open any longer. She snapped a few photos for us, and I had her send them to me on my phone. These amazing people were going to be his grandparents. You could not ask for better role models than the Rhodes.

Shane's smile was infectious as he walked over to his father to take Wyatt from his arms. He whispered that he would put him to bed and would be right back down. Kip did a big exaggerated stretch of his arms and then winked at me.

"It's been a long time since I've done that. I almost forgot how it feels to tend to a little one. He may be seven, but he fits perfectly in my arms."

"I know what you mean. I took him to Tenley's pediatrician, and he said he's under on the growth and weight scale, but since he's been here, he's probably gained a few pounds. I just pray it will be permanent."

"I hope you get your wish, I really mean that. I just can't bear to see you and Shane disappointed."

"We understand that more than you know, but thank you, Kip. We love you and are not sure what we would do without you and Kathleen."

"Well, don't worry about that, because we don't plan on going anywhere anytime soon." My mother-in-law said as she walked back into the living room. "Okay, love, it's late and ranch work won't get done, especially if my cowboy over here is tired."

"I'm coming, woman, and when have I ever not done ranch work?"

"Never, but I have to keep you on your toes now. Good night, Shelby. Talk with you in the morning."

I hugged her back and then gave one more to Kip before they left. I picked up a little in the living room and then wondered what was keeping Shane. I went upstairs and heard him talking to Wyatt, but he was still asleep.

"It's going to be alright buddy, I have to believe that. You came into our lives like a breeze on a windy day. Sometimes life throws you a curveball, and something so unexpected comes into your life that you may not know what to do with it, but with you, I never felt that way. Something just clicked inside of me when I looked into your eyes, and I wished you were ours. A son that I could claim as my own and be a father to, and now it's not just a dream anymore, it's a reality. I promise you, Wyatt, if you want me to be your dad, then I promise I will be the best one I can be and will always love and put you and your mom first. Yeah, that's Shelby, the pretty blonde that makes my head spin.

Yeah, she's pretty great. Okay, good night, buddy. Dream of things that will make you smile."

I watched Shane place a kiss down on his forehead, and I nearly melted. It was a beautiful moment he just had with Wyatt, and although I shouldn't have been listening, I'm so happy I did, because now I knew how Shane felt. I knew he wanted Wyatt to be our son, but I never knew how much until now. I wanted to run back downstairs, but I was caught when Shane stepped out of his room.

"I'm not even sorry for eavesdropping," I said and then laughed in his arms.

"I somehow knew you were there, and that's okay. Shelby, I don't think I can let him go, so we have to make sure everything goes right for us on Monday."

"It will, babe. It has to. I have faith, and I know you do too. Look how much he's changed since we took him in. His cheeks are rosy. The dark circles under his eyes are gone, and he never stops smiling. This is right. I know it is."

"Just keep telling me that until we sign the papers."

"I will. Let's go to bed. I need my husband."

"Lead the way, wife."

I had spent a wonderful week with Wyatt, and it was Shane's turn to show him around the ranch and just do guy stuff. I couldn't help but let out my laughter after they both came down the stairs the next morning. Shane had dressed him almost identical to him, right down to his cowboy boots. It was really hard containing my joy around these two, especially mornings like this one when we could not have asked for a better day.

After talking to Shane about it, I decided to let the dust settle with Tenley and waited a few days to talk to her. After I received the call this morning from Judge Clayton's office confirming our hearing for Monday morning, I knew it was now or never to get it all out on the table.

"May I come in?" I asked as a stunned Tenley opened her door.

"Did we have an appointment?" she asked, surprised.

"No, but we do need to talk. Can we?"

"I have a few minutes while Jamie is napping. Do you want some coffee? I just made a fresh pot."

"Coffee sounds great. Thank you."

"It's no trouble at all," she said as she pulled two mugs down from the cabinet. "Would you like a muffin? I made them yesterday morning. They should still be fresh."

I watched her busy herself around her kitchen while I remained standing by the kitchen island. She was not the easiest person to talk to on a normal day. *Yeah, this could be an epic mistake on my part, but I'll just add it to the list.*

"Seriously, Tenley, can you just sit and talk to me? The air is so thick in the room right now that I'm finding it hard to breathe. The coffee and the muffins can wait. What I need to talk to you about will not."

She placed the serving tray down and placed her palms down on the counter, looking directly at me as if she did not know why I was here.

I took my coat off and then walked into the living room and took a seat on the couch. I figured I would make myself comfortable and ready for this conversation. She followed suit but still said nothing, just gesturing me to continue.

"Tenley, you can tell me that you're angry with me, and I'll listen, but it won't change the fact on what I asked of you, and then without telling me, you just went ahead and did it."

"I don't know what you're talking about, Shelby, and I'm not sure what you want me to say here."

"How about the truth? I need to know that whatever you did for us to help us secure our boy will not come back to haunt us and jeopardize our adoption of Wyatt."

I would have thought after the bombshell I just dropped on her, she would have had a reaction, but she was cool as a cucumber. She kept her expression on the serious side and picked off the imaginary lint from her leggings before looking up at me.

"I told you the truth, Shelby. It's not my problem that you don't believe me. I am a lawyer, and as your lawyer, I did everything I know to do to begin the adoption process for Wyatt. I told you there were special circumstances that were taken into consideration, and some of those processes were pushed to the head of the line, which in turn expedited your hearing. If I were you, I would not question the why and the how and just be happy that when Monday comes, you will be that much closer to becoming Wyatt's family."

I didn't know what to say, and when the words were there, the sound of baby Jamie crying through the monitor broke up the already high tension in the room. Tenley didn't miss a beat and reached for the monitor. She stood and began walking toward the stairs. I was still planted on the couch in total astonishment to what was said and wasn't said here today. The heavy unspoken understanding between us was right there and the way she was looking at me was scaring the shit out of me. Tenley didn't play, especially when she was in lawyer mode.

"So, as you can hear, my little boy needs me. If there's nothing else, you should go home to yours."

Yeah, it didn't take a genius to figure out that I was being shown the door.

Without thought, I reached for Tenley and hugged her with every bit of gratitude I had in me. There would never be enough thank you's for all she did to make my dream come true, but then again, according to Tenley, she was just doing the job I hired her for and anything beyond that was just my imagination. It would be up to me how I handle the acceptance of it all and move on from here.

"Thank you, Tenley, thank you."

"Take care, Shelby." She turned away and walked up the stairs to be with her son, and I did the same by driving home to mine. Tenley was right about the dream. We were so close to having it, and I made a promise to myself not to question it.

By the time I got back to our place, Shane was finished for the day. He was out in the barn with Wyatt, Luke, and Wade. Wyatt was holding one of the big rakes and trying with all his best effort to muck up Yankee's stall. Why was this so awesome to witness? I smiled, and then Shane walked over and took me in his arms.

"Hey, baby, where have you been?" he asked and then kissed me so passionately that I would feel it for days.

"Someone is in a good mood. How was your day, Shane?"

"Amazing. The new quarter horses arrived this morning. My dad and Ren have been working them out on the south ridge. Brock almost fell over when I was able to acquire all eight that were up for auction, but you know me and my negotiating skills."

"I do, and your smile says it all. So, I see you have put Wyatt to work. How's he doing?"

"He loves it and is a natural cowboy. I put him on Joker today, and I think they are best friends, which is a miracle in itself because that horse only has his name because of his past wild days. But to watch him welcome Wyatt the way he did, well, babe, I was in awe. Are you going to tell me where you went? Or am I going to continue to rattle on here?"

"Ask me again later. For now, I just want to be here with my guys. Is that okay?"

"Yeah, baby, it's more than okay; it's everything."

When it was time to put Wyatt to bed, Shane raced him up the stairs to his room. I trailed behind them and declared Wyatt the winner when Shane slowed down for him to pass him. Every moment we have spent with this little boy has been amazing, and I never wanted the feeling to end, but after today, I was scared if it might be too much for Wyatt. While he was brushing his teeth, I asked Shane if we could talk alone for a minute.

"What's up?"

"Shane, I don't want to burst the bubble here—Lord knows I love it—but something just occurred to me as I watched you with him."

"What? Come on, babe, you're scaring me."

"We know what we want, but has either one of us asked Wyatt what he wants? We jumped over a lot of steps here, and now with the hearing in two days, it's really hitting me. I'm sorry, maybe it's my talk with Tenley today, but I just need Monday to be perfect, but more so I need Wyatt to want to be here. He has to want us for his parents, and it feels as if we have been playing house."

"Okay, what do you want to do?"

"What we should have done before we started all of this. We need to talk to him and ask Wyatt what he wants, because no one has ever put him first. We have to be sure before Monday."

19

Making a family

Shane

"You're right, Shelby. We have to talk to him."

"Okay, let's put him to bed, and tomorrow we will talk."

I kissed Shelby on her forehead and breathed my beautiful wife in, while I was silently praying that we would finally get our happily ever after with Wyatt. Then we really would be a family.

"Okay, little man, hop up, and I will tuck you in like a burrito."

"What's a burrito?" he asked with his curious brown eyes.

"Shelby, please tell this boy what a burrito is and how it is needed in his life."

"Well, if you haven't figured it out yet by Shane's excitement, he loves burritos. The outside of the burrito is called a tortilla. It's like a round flat thin bread. You can stuff it with meat, vegetables, and cheese. After you fill it with what you like, you just fold it over or roll it, and voila! You have yourself a burrito. And what Shane meant about tucking you in like one goes something like this." I watched Shelby tuck in the covers really tight around Wyatt, while he laughed.

"Okay, you are now a burrito. How do you feel?" she asked.

"I can't move."

"Yup, that's the idea."

He wiggled and loosened the blankets and then did something I didn't expect. He sat up and hugged Shelby, and then reached for me to join in on the hug. He was so small in between the two of us, and as his little arms were around our necks, I think we had our answer on what Wyatt wanted. I kissed him on the top of his head and quickly wiped away my tears. I hadn't felt this happy in a really long time. The next morning, Shelby and I practically jumped out of bed, excited to spend every waking minute with Wyatt.

"So, who wants seconds?" Shelby asked as she plated the rest of the French toast and sausage. We both raised our hands and shouted "Me!" and then Wyatt said I could have the French toast if he could have the sausage.

We compromised and split everything equally. Before he took another bite, I raised my fork and he did the same, and then I said, "Give me some fork," which made him laugh.

We clinked our utensils and then dug into our pile of food. In just a short time, he had come to life living with us. I looked over at Shelby, and she knew it was time to talk to him.

"Hey, Wyatt, can we talk for a minute?" I asked.

"Sure! If it's about mucking up the stalls, I'll do it for you."

"It's not, but thank you. Any kind of help is always appreciated, especially in the barn."

After I hesitated for a bit, Shelby came over and stood beside me. Wyatt's happy expression fell a bit, but he just sat there quietly, waiting for me to talk. I let out a breath and then simply pulled off the Band-aid.

"Wyatt, do you like living here?"

"I love it. It's the most beautiful place on earth."

"Yeah, it's pretty special, but what I want to know is if you're happy living with us." I reached for Shelby's hand and linked it with mine. "Because we really like having you here, but we need to know how you feel."

He looked all around the kitchen and then back to us before answering our question. "Are you sending me back?"

"No, Wyatt, we want you here with us. We want you as our son. And we—Shelby and I—will be your mom and dad, if that's what you want."

"I really don't have to go back to the home?"

"No, not if you don't want to. You never have to go back to that place again."

"What about Mrs. Rosie? Will I be able to see her again?"

"Um, we can talk about it and maybe arrange a visit once we meet her. Wyatt, what do you think about the question I asked you? How do you feel about us becoming your parents? Is that okay?"

"I never had a mommy or a daddy."

"Well, you do now. That is…if you want to."

Oh, my god! I feel like I'm going to throw up. Shelby let me take the lead on this because she knew she would cry all the way through it, but damn, this is hard. I feel as if we are laying down our entire future in his little hands, and his answer will decide our fate.

He climbed down the stool and gave me a hug. I was a tall man, over six feet in height, so he measured up to my thigh. I placed my hand on his back, and then Shelby joined in for a group hug.

"I love you, daddy."

It took everything I had inside of me not to break down in front of him, but that didn't stop Shelby. I lifted him in my arms and hugged him with all that I had and prayed he felt my love—our love—for him.

Shelby was right. I was over questioning fate. We were a family, the three of us, and the next time I visited Jamie, I'd thank him for sending Wyatt to us.

The doorbell interrupted our moment, and Shelby went to answer the door while I stayed back to hug our son.

"Shane!" she called out.

I put Wyatt down and held his hand as I made my way to the door.

"Mrs. Rosie! You found me," he happily said and then ran into the arms of the stranger standing in our doorway. She wasn't alone though. Tenley was here, along with another woman.

"Let me look at you, Wyatt. Oh, have you gotten taller?"

"Maybe. They feed me a lot of pancakes."

Mrs. Rosie laughed and then gave him a hug. She was older but not what I had pictured based on how he described her.

"Hey, it's cold out there. Please, come into our home," I said and then gestured for everyone to go into the living room.

We had a fire going, which Wyatt loved. He took a seat by the fire, and Mrs. Rosie sat beside him on the chair.

"So, what's this all about?" I asked Tenley.

She placed her briefcase down and asked if we could speak privately and without Wyatt. I felt sick to my stomach. Something wasn't right here, and I still don't know who the other woman was. I was speechless, so was Shelby, and then the front door opened, and it was Jagger.

"Hey, who wants to ride Joker?" he asked and then clapped his hands together.

"Me!" Wyatt said, practically springing to his feet and over to Jagger. "I can really ride Joker again?"

"Well, not by yourself, but it should be fun."

"Can I, daddy?" he turned back and asked.

All eyes in the room were on me. It was so quiet you could hear a pin drop. This was the second time he called me daddy, and it just made me want to cry and drop to my knees on how great it felt.

I cleared my throat and simply said, "Sure you can. Listen to Jagger, okay?"

"I will." He put his coat on and then came back over to Mrs. Rosie. "Will you be here when I get back?" The look on her face told me no, but she said nothing in return and just hugged Wyatt and told him to have fun.

After the front door closed, Tenley interrupted my thoughts.

"Okay, let's all take a breath and have a seat. Shane, Shelby, I would like you to meet Roberta Davidson. She is a friend of mine and a caseworker for family services. She works closely with Judge Clayton and will be overseeing Wyatt's adoption."

"Hi, a pleasure to meet you. This is my wife, Shelby."

"Hello, Shane and Shelby. Please, there is no need to fear my presence here. I know you are probably wondering why I'm here when your hearing is on Monday, but this is the first opportunity I have had to meet you, and I have wanted to. I also wanted to formally introduce you to Rosie, Wyatt's grandmother."

We gasped. "Grandmother? We thought you were a volunteer at the group home," I said and then took a seat as Shelby's grip tightened on my hand.

"I do volunteer at the group home. It's my way of remaining close to my grandson."

"Forgive me for being blunt, but if he's your grandson, then why is he living at the group home and not with you? And why does he call you Mrs. Rosie if you're his family?"

"He doesn't know that I'm his grandmother, and I would like to keep it that way. I don't have the means to care for him, and I am not in the best of health. I never knew my daughter had gotten pregnant, or the fact that she gave him up. I only discovered this about nine months ago. After months of searching, I found out that he was here in Wyoming, and recently back at the group home for children. I just wanted to make sure he was okay, and then after spending some time with him, I couldn't just walk out and never see him again. So, I became a volunteer and visited the home when I could."

"Why don't you want him to know who you really are?"

"Mr. Rhodes…"

"Call me Shane."

"Fine, Shane. I can't hurt him with the truth, so I lie to protect him. My daughter is a train wreck, but she did one right thing in her life, and that was giving up that boy for a chance at a better life. I know living in an orphanage is not that dream, but it's better than the alternative. I haven't spoken to my daughter in years, and if you ask me if she's alive, I won't be able to say. I only found out about Wyatt missing last week, but it has taken me this long to find the courage to come out here. I was so upset when I heard he took off from his group, but then again, I wasn't really surprised by it. He was so unhappy in that place, and all he wanted was a family, but it wasn't anything I could give to him. So I kept on going back to visit and be as close as I could to him."

"So what happens now? Will you try to stop our adoption of Wyatt?"

"No, I will not. I can see how much he has changed in the short time he's been with you, and to hear him call you daddy is music to my ears. You have given him what he has always wanted, and that's a family. No one will stand in your way of that happening. I have to get going, but I have signed all the necessary papers you'll need for Monday. Although my daughter forfeited her rights, now that I've come forward as his next of kin, I have had to do the same."

"Are you sure?"

"Yes, it's the right thing to do for Wyatt. Rest assured, I will not stand in your way. The only thing I ask is if I may come back to see him again before I leave for my trip."

"Of course, just tell us when."

"I'll have Roberta here arrange that for me, and when it's set, I'll be here."

I was stunned and in complete shock, and I think Shelby was too. We walked Mrs. Rosie out, and then we joined Tenley back in the living room with the social worker.

Roberta explained, "I know it's a lot to take in and all at once, but it was quite the revelation for me as well. I've known Rosie for a long time now, and I never connected the dots that she was related to Wyatt. I've met a lot of people in my line of work, with each story being very different from the other. I've learned not to question most of them and just do my job to the best of my ability. Thanks to your lawyer here, everything I would have done over a course of time has been done at a rapid speed, but it was Judge Clayton that signed off on this case, and he is one judge you never argue with. So, I'm going to leave this paperwork with you to read and sign for me. You can give me the file on Monday when we meet with Judge Clayton."

"Excuse me, but are you telling us that after Monday, Wyatt will be our son? He will legally be our son?" I asked.

"Yes, is there another way I don't know about?"

"No, I guess not. I'm just trying to wrap my brain around this."

"Yeah, me too. Again, Mr. Rhodes, there are some things I don't question, and this is one of those times. I'll see you all on Monday."

"I'll walk you out," Tenley said, and then she walked Roberta out to her car, leaving just Shelby and I, staring at each other.

"Oh my god, Shane, is this really happening?"

"Yeah, baby, I think it is."

"I can't believe that woman is his grandmother. It must be killing her to walk away from him."

"No, not as bad as knowing she would be leaving him to the state," said Tenley, as she walked back into the room.

"Why, Tenley? We need to know." I asked.

"No, what you need to do is read this file and sign the papers. His medical file is also included. Thankfully, he's up to date on his vaccinations, and for a young child, he's hardly ever been sick. Everything you need is in there. Birth certificate, social security card, medical, and family history. There's not much on that, but as far as I know from Rosie, they don't have any genetic cancers or any significant heart issues, diabetes, etc."

"What's wrong with Rosie?" Shelby asked.

"She has lung cancer, stage four. It's pretty sad. The poor woman worked two jobs her entire life, providing for her family, and she never smoked a day in her life. It says she worked for a chemical company, and it's due to longtime exposure. During the time Wyatt ran away, she was down in Denver at the Cancer Treatment Center."

"How much time does she have left?"

"A few months, maybe less."

"Tenley, I don't know the right words to express how thankful we are to you for helping us. I still can't believe this is real."

"Shane," she began to say, and then looked over to Shelby, and then back to me. "Just be the best parents you can be for that little boy. That's all the thanks I need. Okay, I have to go. I'll see you on Monday."

Shelby practically jumped into my arms, and as I held her, I looked over to my friend. Tenley mouthed the words "I love you" and then walked out, closing the door behind her.

"This is real, Shane. We are going to be a family, and Wyatt is going to be our son. Oh my god, Shane, I'm so happy." She cried, and then at that very moment, Wyatt was back from riding and running happily toward us with the rosiest cheeks we had ever seen. I watched Shelby take him into her arms and listen to his animated story about riding with Jagger and how much he loved Joker.

"Will you be alright on your own? I just want to walk Jagger out," I asked.

"Sure, we're fine," she happily said and then hugged Wyatt before helping him out of his coat.

Jagger waited for me while I had another happy moment with Shelby and Wyatt, and then I grabbed my coat and walked out with him.

"Talk to me, man. How is this all happening?" I asked.

"It's not for me to tell you, brother. It's up to Tenley."

"Come on, Jagger, what does that even mean? I can't have any surprises when we go before the judge on Monday."

"Shane, there won't be. You have to trust Tenley. She knows what she's doing, and when it's all over, you are going to walk out of that courthouse on Monday as a father to Wyatt. Your dream has finally come true. Don't stand here and fucking question it. Just be grateful.

Leave it at that."

"Yeah, I hear you, man, but I have to protect my family and that boy in there. He is so happy right now and so is Shelby. I have to know that it's not just going to be ripped out from under us. We've lived through that too many times, and I can't go through it again. We won't survive it, Jagger. You should know; you bore witness to it."

"I promise you that Tenley would never allow that to happen. If you don't believe me, then look up at the sky tonight, and he'll be there waiting for you."

I knew what Jagger meant, and he knew how I felt. I trusted him and Tenley with my life, and I knew without a doubt that they would move heaven and earth for me if it meant for our dream to come true. She did that for me today, and so much of me wanted to just ask her how she pulled it off, but after she looked at Shelby, I knew I might never know, and I guess I would have to be okay with that. People have lived with worse, and this was not anything that came close to that. This was a miracle and the very best gift we could ever be so lucky to receive. I didn't need to challenge fate and seek out the divine intervention I needed in the past, because I felt it in every part of my being.

Shelby fell asleep smiling, and Wyatt did too. It was a perfect day, just the three of us spending time together.

I wore many hats in this life, sometimes too many, but I had never been more prepared to take on the role as a father to Wyatt. With all that I had accomplished in my life, nothing came as close to perfection as the feeling I felt that washed over me tonight when I read Wyatt a bedtime story.

Right before he closed his eyes, he whispered, "I love you, daddy."

20

Dreams do come true

Shane

I was never one to observe Sunday as a day of rest, not in a rancher's life, but today was different. I didn't ever remember a time when I slept in, but again, today was different.

My beautiful wife was still asleep beside me, and I wasn't sure if her smile from the night before ever faded. Shelby was a natural beauty, never needing a lot of makeup to enhance what she was born with. And when she was at peace, that's when she never looked more beautiful. Her long eyelashes were sweeping across her face, and her nose would twitch every once in a while, and that's when I knew she was dreaming of something happy.

It was just about eight o'clock when I finally got up from our warm bed. I'd been watching her for hours and appreciating the life I still had with her. I didn't want to live in the past and relive over and over again the hurt that had dragged us down. We had much to live for, and now with Wyatt in our lives, it gave all the more reason to move forward.

I slowly opened the door to the guest room which would be transformed into our little boy's room after tomorrow. He was asleep wrapped up in blankets and with good old Tinker beside him. Tink was a golden retriever whom we rescued about six years back. He'd been a great friend to our family in the times we really needed one, and I wasn't so sure how much life he had left in him, but with the arrival of an energetic seven-year-old, he seemed reborn and had taken over the role as his best friend. He raised his head up in a protective stance, and then he came over to me for praise.

"Good boy, you keep an eye on Wyatt, okay?" He didn't bark, just gave me the look of understanding and took his place beside Wyatt's bed.

I skipped making the coffee and just headed straight to the barn to saddle up Yankee. I had so much life in my lungs this morning, and I knew the moment my boots hit the bottom floor, a long ride was calling my name.

I made it to the oak tree, the very same tree where Jamie had tried to explain for me all of life's meanings in his whimsical ways. While Yankee drank from the river, I placed my palms against the tree and closed my eyes to bring me back to that day with Jamie. I would do anything to hear his voice again.

I felt my body slowly lowering to the ground, and then with my palms still against the tree, I placed my forehead on it and prayed.

"I need you, Jamie, more than I ever have before. It feels as if my faith has been restored in all things, and I don't even know how to begin to say thank you for this gift I have been given. Please, Jamie, give me some kind of sign to tell me that everything is going to be okay tomorrow. It's not just a dream, it's a reality."

I don't know what I was expecting to happen right then and there, but I turned and sat down on the cold, hard ground and closed my eyes. Yankee was in his glory just relaxing by the river, while I breathed in the clean mountain air and reflected for a bit before heading back home.

When my body finally relaxed, a force of energy swept through me. I felt as if I was flying. My eyes blinked open, and that's when I saw him walking toward me through the mist coming off the water. I closed my eyes again and willed whatever hallucination was happening to me to just go away, but then I heard his voice. I wasn't transported back into a comforting memory in my past. He was here with me now.

"Jamie? How are you here?" I said, and then sprang up to my feet and looked all around me, but no one else was here. It was just Jamie.

"Don't you know, Shane?"

I could hardly catch my breath, and then instead of answering his question, I just closed my eyes again, not believing for one second that this was real.

"Open your eyes, Shane. Look at me."

I heard his voice as clear as day, and then my eyes opened as if I no longer had control over them. They were staring right back at my best friend and brother.

"There you are. Now, back to your question. I'm here because you called for me from the deepest part of your heart and soul. I don't do this often. It's not as easy as you think, so let's make this time count."

"Jamie, I'm out of my fucking mind right now."

"Watch your mouth, the big guy upstairs frowns on that."

"Oh my…"

"Whoa! He doesn't like that either."

"Sorry," I found myself saying, and then I shook my head trying to shake the crazy from my mind.

"So, now that we have that out of the way, let's talk. I have a clock on me, so I'm going to tell you what you think you need to hear."

"Jamie, of all the times I have prayed for you, I can't believe this is happening right now. Of all the people you could have dropped in on, you choose me. Why?"

"You needed me the most, it's that simple. I hear your prayers. It's kind of hard turning it off. I'm not going to explain how it all works. I think you already know. If you truly didn't believe, then I surely would not be here right now."

"It's really you?"

"Yeah, brother, I'm here."

Without another thought, I reached for Jamie and pulled him into a bone-crushing hug. I didn't want him to go. He looked the same. He sounded the same. He was here because I needed him to be. *What did I say before about divine intervention? Yeah, that theory is moot at this point.*

We walked down by the river, and as we got closer to the water, Yankee kicked up on his hind legs and neighed aloud. Did he sense Jamie here too? As Jamie got closer to the horse, a calm washed over Yankee, and he nudged into Jamie's shoulder. I had never seen anything like this and probably would never be able to make anyone understand what my eyes were seeing today. This was a miracle having Jamie here with me.

"There now, settle down, boy. Yeah, you're a good horse," he said as he ran his hand down his neck. "So, let's get to it. I don't have too much time left. You remember the last time we were down by this river, don't you, Shane?"

"I do. It was the best day with you and also the hardest because I knew time was running out, and then you died."

"Yeah, I did, and believe me when I say it was not easy to leave all of you, but it was just my time, and long before I crossed over to the spirit world, my destiny was already planned out for me. I was given the gift of time when Tenley saved my life. It was only right, in the end, to give Tenley the same gift. As you can see, it all worked out, because she's happily married to Jagger and they have a beautiful son, aptly named after me. It doesn't get better than that. Now, we come to you."

"What about me?"

"Don't you know? You had quite the year running, hiding, and burying all those feelings of yours while the pain and loss of your son just piled on top of you."

"Don't remind me."

"How can I not, when you are still hanging on to it? You say you let it go. Well, prove it. You have this amazing chance to become a father to this beautiful boy, and just watching over Shelby, I know she's higher than the sun in the sky. You need to stop questioning and begin believing. You all think I am an extension of God himself, but I'm not. Sure, it's good for the ego, but I'm simply Jamie. I'm your brother and best friend, and I will always have your back; it's just from another place. There are just some things in life that you may never have the answers to, and that's okay. Tenley made her peace with my dying when she finally allowed herself to let the past go. No one could predict my cancer coming back, just like no one could predict what happened to your son. I will say: Ryder is okay, Shane. I'm looking out for him."

I could not see anything past my tears. Every word Jamie was saying was ripping through my body like a freight train, but not in a bad way. He was giving me peace, the peace he knew I yearned for, and now I finally had it. I wiped my eyes, and then I didn't see him anymore.

"Jamie, Jamie, where are you?" I called out to him.

"I'm here, Shane. Turn around." It was a bright colorful mist with light all around him. It was Jamie. "I have to go, Shane, but I promise you that I am never too far away. Just find my star in the sky, and I'll show you the way. When you can, give my love to my parents and Tenley. Find a way to show Jagger and my little nephew too. And then, tell your son about me and show him our life in pictures. I'm sure he will get a kick out of it. We were just a bunch of kids living and loving life here on this ranch. It's where our soul bleeds into the earth, and it comes alive after the frost melts and the first sign of spring appears. Yeah, tell him about me when you're ready."

"Jamie, I want to tell you…" I got choked up and couldn't find the words to say to him as he slowly faded and floated away from me.

"I know, brother. It's one thing I have always been certain of. Take care of your family. Let them take care of you. It's all going to be alright, I promise you, Shane. I have to go now."

I wiped away my tears and ran as fast as I could toward him, but he just drifted further and further away.

"I love you, Jamie!" I shouted into thin air.

I no longer could see him, but I still felt his strong presence as if he was standing right beside me. I wiped away my tears, and then I heard his final words to me.

"I'll see you in your dreams."

My eyes blinked open, and I looked all around me to find myself completely alone. My horse was still where I left him grazing on the grass. I placed my head back on the tree and then looked up to the sky.

"Yeah, brother, I'll see you in my dreams." And then I left for home to be where I belonged: with Shelby and Wyatt.

My family.

21

the journey begins

Shane

I knew last night when I had finally managed to fall asleep that today would either be the happiest day of our lives or the worst, pending on what the judge says to us. I had been reassured over and over again that we didn't have anything to worry about. Wyatt's grandmother moved forward with relinquishing her rights and had approved us to be Wyatt's adoptive parents.

When Shelby asked if this was real, I gave her the only answer I could, and that was yes. I knew I doubted myself and the legal hoops Tenley jumped through to make this happen. I just wouldn't be calm until we walked out of the courthouse with Wyatt as our son.

I looked at my watch again and ran my fingers through my hair. I was wearing my best suit and traded in the cowboy boots for a pair of loafers. Yeah, I was totally out of my element here with the wardrobe my wife picked out, but I was the agreeable husband and did as she asked. Lord knew our family needed a win, and it had been a long time coming. As we sat in the hallway waiting to be called, I began fidgeting with my watch again.

"Baby, will you stop it? Everything is going to be alright," Shelby said as she placed her hand on mine. "I'm sure they are just running a little late."

Looking over to my parents playing with Wyatt, I tried my hardest to tamper down my anxiety. "Our hearing was supposed to begin fifteen minutes ago. Why hasn't anyone come out to talk to us?"

"I'm not sure, but let's not go there with worry. Let's just try to relax and wait for all parties to arrive." She let out a deep breath as she said it and tightened her hold on my hand. Yeah, she was nervous too and could not hide her feelings from me, but I went along with it for her sake. Just when I was about to lose my mind, I saw Tenley walking toward us with her briefcase in hand.

"Good morning. How are you all doing?" she asked.

"Better, now that you're here. We've been waiting for what seems like forever, and we didn't know what was happening," I practically shouted and then reigned myself back in.

"Shane, the court begins at nine am, and you are first on Judge Clayton's docket. He's never late. You're just early."

Looking at my watch again, I felt totally foolish and then looked back to Tenley, who was practically laughing at me. "Okay, I'm sorry," I said. "I guess we did arrive earlier than we needed to."

"It's fine. Let's start over, okay?" I nodded and then smiled at my friend.

"Good morning, Shelby. How are you doing? Are you nervous like this guy?" Tenley smiled, gesturing right over to me. I wiped my brow, and then she winked at me, giving me her assurance that all would be okay.

"Good morning. No, I'm actually feeling pretty good right now," she said and then stepped up to hug Tenley. They exchanged a few pleasantries, and then it was back to business for Tenley.

"Okay, Roberta is with Judge Clayton. They are in his chambers going over all the paperwork. I can assure you everything is good to go, and I promise you without a doubt in my mind that everything will go accordingly today. You are going to be asked several questions, and then the judge will talk with Wyatt and make his formal ruling. Wyatt is a very smart little boy, and I'm sure the judge will be impressed by him." She was going to say more, but then her phone buzzed in her pocket. "You ready? Because this is it."

My parents walked over and handed off Wyatt to us. My dad looked so happy, growing into his role as a proud grandfather. "We love you, son. You just go in there and show that judge who we are as a family. I've never been prouder."

"Thanks, pop, I needed to hear that. And if I don't say it enough, thank you for showing me the way in times when I had my eyes closed and didn't know if I was coming or going. You have been an amazing role model for me, and I can only hope I will be half the father to Wyatt as you have been for me."

"You'll be better."

Hand in hand, we all walked into the judge's chambers, feeling united as we were about to become a family.

The judge was older in a more distinguished way. He finished reading the file and then took his black framed glasses off and crossed his hands over each other onto his desk.

We all filed in, with Shelby by my side and my parents standing behind me. Tenley was with Roberta, and just as the door began to close, Jagger came barreling in. He was fixing his tie as he nearly tripped over himself. The Fairchild's were next, along with the Parishes. We were practically shoulder to shoulder standing all together in the judge's chambers, but I wouldn't want it any other way. We were this big family, and no matter what, we supported the other. With everyone here with us today, I felt nothing but love and so much pride.

"Come in, come in, please. Everyone, please call attention. Welcome. So, Shane and Shelby Rhodes, you understand by signing this adoption agreement form, you agree to take care of Wyatt as your own legal child?"

"We do."

"You will care for providing for his health, welfare, and educational needs?"

"We do, your honor."

"Wyatt, do you agree to this adoption? Do you want the Rhodes to become your mother and father?"

"Yes! I love them so much, and Joker too!" We all laughed and hugged him.

"Okay, if there isn't anything else to add, let's make this official."

"Your honor, before you do that I would just like to introduce myself. I'm Kip Rhodes, and to my left is my beautiful wife, Kathleen. We are Shane's parents. I just...no, we want to go on record promising you and this court that we will take our role very seriously when it comes to being grandparents to this child. We love him very much, and we will do everything to make sure his life is filled with love, hope, and promises for an amazing life."

I wiped a tear from my eye as Shelby did too. I mouthed "Thank you" to my parents as they stood tall and smiled back over to the judge. He was about to continue, and that's when Brock and Connie introduced themselves and told the judge how happy we all are that Wyatt has come into our lives. He too promised to always be there for my son. Last but not least, Ren and Ellen said their peace, and by the time they finished, the room erupted in tears, laughter, and smiles that could not be contained.

Tenley remained quiet with her silent unshed tears. I knew she was thinking of Jamie and how he was probably looking down on all of us today. When our eyes connected, she smiled and then looked back over to the judge. Jagger squeezed her shoulders, and then he was the last one to state his promises for our son.

"Well, judge, there you have it. This is the only way we know how to be, and that's always united and connected with the love we have for one another. I promise you that I will be the best uncle I know how to be for Wyatt. He's already a cousin to our young son, James Lucas, and I can't wait to show these boys all the amazing things our fathers taught us being raised up on this ranch."

Judge Clayton looked all around his crowded chambers and smiled and looked back over to Wyatt to address him personally.

"It's quite the family you are coming into. Are you ready, son, to make it official?"

"I am!" he shouted excitedly.

"Alright. On this date…" he began to say, "Shane and Shelby Rhodes have officially adopted Wyatt Adam Rhodes. You're now legally their child. You have all the rights to any natural child. I will hereby sign this order confirming the adoption."

The room erupted with applause, tears of joy, and a lot of hugs to go around. We all shook the judge's hands as he wished us well as the new family we had just become.

Shelby could not stop crying as she hugged Wyatt. I wrapped them both in one of my famous bear hugs and said simply, "Let's go home."

I had taken the rest of the week off, and the three of us spent time solely with one another. We were in the winter months, but although it was cold outside, we found so many things to do. We took Wyatt riding along the trails that we used for the campers. We explored Jackson Hole and even went skiing. For a beginner, Wyatt was a natural. Shelby was holding her breath as we eased our way down the bunny trail. Once we reached the bottom, he asked if we could go again. Next to marrying Shelby, and our honeymoon that followed, this was the best week of my life. A memory of my family that I would always cherish.

I had so much to be thankful for, I could hardly find where to begin. I knew I had time to count my blessings. It was just the three of us. We were a family, and life was perfect.

When we resumed our life on the ranch, I began my day with my usual routine. I kissed my beautiful wife goodbye and promised to be back in time for breakfast. Next, I walked into our son's room, where he slept with his faithful companion, Tinker. He just looked up at me with his big brown eyes and moved closer to his boy. I patted Tinker's head and leaned down to kiss my son. I had no worries with Tinker around. He would protect his charge with everything he had in him.

I made my way down to my truck, and there was Jagger waiting for me with a thermos of coffee.

"Am I late?" I asked.

"No, you're right on time. I figured a ride was in order this morning."

"Jag, it's freezing out here, and if you haven't noticed, we have a ranch to run."

"Yup, got it covered. Yankee is ready to go, along with She-devil. You don't want my lady to wait now, do you?" he raised up the thermos to me. I shook my head no and followed my crazy best friend.

I said good morning to my horse. Damn, he was feisty this morning. I made sure everything was secure on Yankee and my pack had everything I needed. I mounted my horse and began our journey to god knows where. Jagger was like the Cheshire cat with the stupid grin he was wearing. I noticed he had more gear than me.

"Just tell me one thing," I inquired.

"Go on."

"We're not going ice fishing again, are we?"

"Maybe," he said, and then he gave She-devil her signal and took off like a bolt of lightning.

I gave him a head start and then motioned to Yankee to do the same. As we rode, I couldn't wait to experience this with Wyatt. He had already taken to ranch life, and along with skiing, he was a natural on a horse. He loved Joker, and the feeling was returned. A boy and his horse: there's nothing better than that.

"Come on, Shane, are you getting slow in your old age?" he called out.

"Fuck you, you wish," I shouted back with Jagger baiting me to accept the challenge. "Let's go, Yankee!" And we were off! It felt like flying anytime I was on my horse, and the feeling never got old for any of us.

We rode to our usual spot down by the river. The horses rested while I enjoyed a cup of coffee to warm myself up.

"Thanks, Jag, for today. It's great up here."

"No need to thank me. You needed this."

"I did?" I said questioningly.

"Yes, you did. We get so caught up in our work here on the ranch that sometimes we forget the fun stuff. I know you just had a great vacation with the family, but this today was for you and me. I remember coming up here after James Lucas was born, and I think I just sat up here all day, thanking the universe for the gift I had been given. I figured you might want to do the same thing."

"I'm a father, Jagger. And it's not a dream!"

"Yes, you are. How does it feel?"

"Amazing," I replied with a smile so wide, my cheeks hurt.

22

Six months later

Shelby

"So, tell me about motherhood. It's been quite the whirlwind for you and for Shane, and now you have a son," said Dr. Whitfield.

It had been a while since I had a one-on-one session with my therapist. Things had been amazing since adopting Wyatt, and I almost didn't want to tempt fate by coming here and rehashing our past.

"It's wonderful, Dr. Whitfield, just the most amazing thing I have in my life."

"And...Shane? How is he adjusting to fatherhood?"

"He's amazing, so hands on with Wyatt. He never said so, but I believe he embraced Wyatt as our son from the moment he found him on our ranch. We had so many signs pointing us in the right direction that we just couldn't question it. I feel whole again. I just can't express it any more than that."

"Shelby, I am very happy for you and for Shane. It seems adopting was a right fit for your family. I guess what I want to know is if you are having any unresolved feelings about losing Ryder to adopting Wyatt."

"I know where this is headed, and I can promise you that I am not doing that. You can't replace children. I will always keep our son in my heart, but I never believed there was no room for anyone else."

"Okay, I believe you. I want you to know that I am always here for you, and for Shane, but it seems I am not needed anymore at this time. I'm very happy for you."

I got up to give her a hug and felt completely right in my decision to complete my therapy. Shane had stopped going months ago, and if he wanted to confide in Wendy, all he had to do was call or visit her. My time with Dr. Whitfield was reserved for me and the things I couldn't say to Shane, at least at first. Now, we were more than okay, and it almost felt perfect.

As I made my way through town, I stopped at the local coffee shop. It was called Beans, a very hip and chic place. It was usually very busy with patrons, especially people that worked in town and near the hospital. I was lucky to catch a parking spot. I ordered my latte and browsed on my phone when a familiar voice called out to me.

"Hi! I thought that was you!"

I turned around to see our caseworker, Roberta. She was also waiting in line and invited me to sit and join her for a minute. Before I could say yes, our orders were called out, and she looked around the café for a table for us.

I didn't move. I felt paralyzed with fear and tried to calm myself down before I made a fool of myself in front of our caseworker. *Who knows how she was reading me at the moment?* This could be a normal reaction for her in the line of work she does. I sipped my latte and she continued on as if we've been friends for years.

"Well, this is a welcomed surprise. I was just thinking of you today and was going to call you once I got back to my office, and now, here you are." She said happily.

I was apprehensive from the moment I heard her voice. It always weighed heavily in the back of my mind how quickly everything was moved along, and I still never knew the role in which Tenley made all that happen. Still, Shane assured me to leave it alone, and I did, right up to this moment.

"Relax, Shelby. You look a little green." She laughed and then took a sip of her coffee.

"Am I that obvious? I guess you took me by surprise."

"As I mentioned, I was going to call you. It's been six months, and I was simply going to check in with you. And to see how Wyatt is doing, especially after Rosie's passing."

I was taken back on the mention of his maternal grandmother. We were deeply saddened when we heard the news of her death. She never did have the opportunity to come back to the ranch to visit Wyatt. She developed an infection shortly after the adoption was finalized and died several days later in the hospital.

"Roberta, let's take a seat." I gestured over to a corner table, and again my apprehension returned. "We never told Wyatt about Rosie, and we feel it's best to continue focusing on our family and our future. He never knew their connection, and he's so young to go through that level of loss."

"Shelby, I understand your reasons to a degree, but to Wyatt, she was his friend. Even if it was for only a short time, she was in his life and he cared about her. Hasn't he wondered why she hasn't been in contact with him?"

"Actually, no. Like I said, we focus on us and not the past." I knew I sounded like a total bitch, but my insides were screaming at me to run home and grab Wyatt before she could take him away.

"If I may offer some advice, I would suggest you re-visit your decision. It is your choice to tell him about Rosie, but I feel it's in his best interest to know the truth. You can decide what that truth will be. He's been through a lot and deserves this chance to finally be a part of a real family, that's all Rosie ever wanted for her grandson. I'm just sorry she is no longer with us to see that happen. Despite the wrong choices her daughter made, Rosie was a good and kind woman. Please keep that in mind. Okay, back to my original question. How is Wyatt?

Does he enjoy school?"

"It took a little time getting him adjusted to school, and then once he was, it was summer time. It's very busy during that time of year on the ranch, but I didn't want him to fall behind again, so I had him tutored the entire summer a couple of days a week, which proved to be instrumentally positive for him. I know it's only second grade, but he is flourishing in his class and he loves his teacher and has already made some good friends."

"Yes, I know, and that is wonderful to hear."

"How do you know?"

"Shelby, I get reports on every area of Wyatt's life for at least the first year of his adoption. It's all been arranged through your lawyer, Tenley Fairchild. I just wanted to ask you personally. It's wonderful to hear how great he is doing. You are a great mom. Furthermore, I will say how thrilled I am with the reports I've been getting. He's perfect for his growth scale, and that makes me so happy. His report card was excellent, and I received a few family pictures that are now hanging on my 'Hall of Fame Wall' down at my office. I could not be happier for you."

"Thank you." I could barely pass the words over my lips. I was reeling from this unexpected but friendly encounter when all I intended to do was get a coffee and return home to my happy life. Sitting here with Roberta made me feel as if I was under the microscope.

She looked down at her watch and then finished off her coffee. "It's getting late and I have appointments this afternoon. How about I stop by early next week? I will have my assistant call you."

"Sure, I'll make it happen."

"Great, and I would like to speak with Shane and Wyatt too."

"Um, Wyatt will be in school. Can it be just us?"

"Unfortunately, no. Home visits include all parties involved. Please don't stress about it. I know everything is fine. This is just routine. I have to run."

It took everything for me to fight the bile rising in my throat. I called home to the ranch and asked Kathleen to pick up Wyatt from the bus stop. There was someone I needed to see before going home. Her office wasn't too far from the coffee shop. I knew she worked in town several days a week, and just my luck today was the right day. I didn't want any scenes at her home, and I prayed I could keep my emotions in check at her office. I hoped she would see me since I was dropping in without an appointment. I loved Tenley as a sister and tried hard to make amends with her since adopting Wyatt. She always gave me the same answer anytime I broached the uncomfortable subject with her about our argument and the harsh things I said to her.

She repeatedly warned me to forget about it and move on. I tried very hard to do that. With unexpectedly seeing Roberta today, all those insecurities were back, and I just needed to talk to her.

I was on her turf now, and it could be very intimidating. Shane said that when she's in her lawyer zone, she can be difficult and not always welcoming. Let's hope that was not true today. I stepped off the elevator to her floor and walked down the long corridor. Once I was inside, I was greeted by her personal assistant.

"Hello, may I help you?" she asked politely enough and right to the point.

"Yes, I'm Shelby Rhodes, a friend of Ms. Fairchild's. Is she in?"

"She is, but with a client. She should be finished in about twenty minutes or so. Do you mind waiting?"

"I don't mind."

"Great. I'll pass her a note and let her know you are here. May I offer you a beverage while you wait?"

"No, thank you. I'm fine."

I took a seat on one of the two soft leather couches that were in the guest lounge. Her office was gorgeous. Fine art was displayed along the walls, and because her office was on the top floor, the windows displayed the morning and afternoon sun with gorgeous mountain views in the background.

I texted Shane that I was still running errands and not to worry. He

159

responded quickly and told me everything was covered at home. I knew that once I arrived home I would have to explain my run-in with Roberta and my impromptu visit with Tenley.

After nearly forty minutes of waiting, Tenley finally emerged from her office. She barely glanced over my way and then said her goodbyes to her smiling clients. After they stepped onto the elevator, she talked with her assistant and then walked back into her office.

"Mrs. Rhodes, Ms. Fairchild needs to take an overseas call. Do you mind waiting?"

This was bullshit! But I was the one that showed up on her doorstep, so I agreed and sat back down. Lucky for me, her call only took an additional ten minutes, and then I was told to go in. She was typing away on her laptop when I took a seat in front of her desk.

"Be right with you. I just have to finish this e-mail and then... send. Okay, now that that's done, hello, Shelby. What can I do for you?"

"Hi, Tenley. Can we drop the formalities and just talk? I need a friend now, not a lawyer."

She leaned back in her chair and said, "Well, in case you forgot, I am both to you, and you are interrupting my workday. So, if you wanted a personal conversation, then we could have this back at my home or your home, not here in my downtown office."

"Point made as ever. Okay, you got me. I was in town after an appointment, and I ran into Roberta at the coffee shop."

"And? What does that have to do with me?"

"It doesn't, until the subject of Wyatt came up. Why didn't you tell me that you are providing reports to her office about my family?"

"As your lawyer, it is my job to maintain a relationship with the state on your behalf. I am also friends with Roberta, and although your adoption of Wyatt has been finalized and closed, it is not unheard of to periodically check in with the adoptive family within the first calendar year. And, for your information, it's not a secret. You have been given copies of everything I have sent to her office. Do you even look through your mail?" Tenley's tone was almost mocking.

"I guess I've been too busy being a mother to Wyatt. I will read them when I get home," I snapped back.

"I'm a mother as well, and a very busy one. Get to your point of this visit. I really need to get back to work, so I can return home to my son."

"Tenley, it always seems we get off on the wrong foot, and that's probably my fault, but seeing Roberta today took me by surprise. She asked me if I had told Wyatt about Rosie, and I don't think she was happy that I chose not to tell him about her death."

"Look, that's your decision, yours and Shane's. I reserve no judgment on that subject. The only thing I have done is provide the standard requirement to her office. She's more than pleased with Wyatt's acclimation and progress. In another six months, you will never have to see or speak with her again, if you choose to do so."

"So, when she visits the ranch next week, will you be there?"

"In what capacity? Personal or professional?"

"A little bit of both, I guess."

"Let me know when, and I will check my schedule. Do yourself a favor and try to relax and just behave accordingly as if it was any other day. She's on your side, and so am I, for that matter. When are you going to realize that?"

"I apologize. I won't take up any more of your time." I got up to leave, and that's when she stopped me.

"Shelby, I'm not the enemy here. I never was. Please remember that the next time you hug your precious little boy."

I could hardly breathe. My mind reeled in a million directions at the hidden meaning she was trying to get across to me. Once my voice returned, I managed to say, "I will," and then I got out of there as fast as my feet could take me.

I had always known there was more to Tenley than meets the eye, and although she said she was no longer the person she once was while in New York, her words today obliterated that. I knew without a doubt

that Tenley Fairchild did the impossible and made my dream of becoming a mother a reality. I also knew she was not one to be crossed
and also could have the power to decimate my life if she wanted to.
After Shane confronted me after speaking with Tenley, he was angry
with me but not enough where he couldn't forgive me for what I had
done. I was never quite sure how much Shane knew of my confronta-
tion with Tenley. He was angry about my asking her to bend the rules
in our favor, but he never said more than that. I knew bringing up
something so personal about Shane to Tenley was wrong, and one
point, I believed he may have known and just chose never to tell me
until I saw the look on Tenley's face today, and it was confirmed.

She never told him. She protected Shane, her best friend, and his
feelings. In choosing to remain quiet, she also protected me. I was such
a bitch to Tenley, and she never deserved it.

God! I hated to feel this way about someone Shane loved and
cared about so much. It made me feel weak and petty with all my insecurities rising up to the surface again.

My nerves were just rattled after seeing and talking to Roberta. I
was totally fine up until that moment, and I would be again. Tenley
was right. I just had to relax and behave as I had been…happy.

As I pulled up to our house, Shane was tossing the football to Wyatt, as Kip and Jagger were talking on our porch. I let out a calming
breath and put on my best smile to greet my boys.

"Mommy!" Wyatt shouted excitedly.

"Hey, baby, how was your day?" I asked as I scooped him up into
my arms.

"It was great. Grandma surprised me at the bus stop and took me
for ice cream before coming home."

"She did? Ice cream before dinner?"

"Oops! I wasn't supposed to tell you that." He laughed, and then I
laughed too.

"It's okay. I won't tell. Why don't you go inside and wash up for
dinner, okay?"

"Okay, mommy." He gave me another hug and then tossed the football back to Shane.

"Game over, daddy! Rematch tomorrow?"

"You know it!" Shane called out. "Hey, you, where have you been? I'm starving."

"For?"

"You have to ask?" he kissed me soundly on my lips, and then our audience was hooting and hollering behind us.

"I guess I know, but after your entourage leaves and a certain seven-year-old is sound asleep up in his room."

"I can't wait."

I chatted with Kip and Jagger for a few minutes, and then Kip walked down to the barn with Shane to look over one of our new horses. Jagger was about to leave himself, and then I asked if I could speak with him for a minute.

"Jagger, I saw Tenley today at her office."

"And? Everything okay?"

"You tell me."

"Shelby, I'm not too sure on what you are asking?"

"I know I'm supposed to play deaf, dumb, and blind when it comes to Tenley and how our adoption was expedited, but I'm worried, Jagger. I always worry that the bottom is going to just fall out from under us and we are going to lose Wyatt. Please, this is not for me, because I know I don't deserve it. I'm asking for Shane. Tell me that I'm wrong and everything is as perfect as the day we took Wyatt home as our son."

"Shelby, I don't know what brought this on, and I don't want to know. Everything is fine and as it should be. I don't know what your hang-ups are with my wife, but that's your issue to resolve. And as for you not deserving? You have everything you always wanted. Why do you question it?"

"Why? Because I'm scared, Jagger. Haven't you ever been scared of anything before? Afraid of losing what you love most in life?"

"Yeah, I have, and I've experienced it as well, along with Shane. We lost Jamie. For a long time, we lost our friendship, and then I lost Tenley for five long years. So, yes, I've been scared, but even with all those truths I have had to face in my life, there has also been so much good. It's okay to have these feelings, but it's another thing to allow them to take over your life. Shelby, please, for the sake of your family, you need to let this go. We're family, and at the end of the day, that's what matters. Tenley and I love you guys so much; let that be enough reason to let go of the mistrust and speculation. Can you do that?"

"I can. I'm sorry, Jagger. I thought I had, and then seeing the caseworker today brought it all back for me."

He stepped up closer and brought me in for a hug. I couldn't stop my tears from falling. He stroked my hair and whispered in my ear, "Shelby, no one will ever take your son away from you and Shane. I promise you."

"Hey!" Shane called out. "What's going on? You okay, babe?"

I stepped out of Jagger's arms and into Shane's. "Oh, hush now. I was having a moment, and Jagger here was just being a friend. A best friend."

Shane visibly calmed and then kissed me on my forehead.

"Thanks, man." Shane said. The two best friends shook hands, and then Jagger made his way home, leaving me alone with my husband.

"Come on, baby, why the tears?"

"I ran into Roberta this afternoon after my appointment, and the entire visit just rattled me. Then old anxieties resurfaced, and I found myself in Tenley's office."

"Oh, babe, no! Why would you do that?"

"I don't know, Shane. I feel so foolish to allow my self-doubt to freak me out again. I'm just scared. I know what I asked of Tenley, and then it suddenly happened. Haven't you ever wondered why that is?"

"Yes, I have, but I'm also smart enough not to question it. I've learned the hard way so many times in my life and got burned for it. I get it, believe me when I say that I do, but it's over and behind us. We have him, and he's not going anywhere. No one is going to threaten our family or ever take our son from us. Shelby, you need to just trust. Roberta is on our side as well as Tenley. Please stop vilifying her as the enemy. She's our friend, and we are lucky to have her in our life."

"Okay, subject dropped. I'm sorry."

"Good. Let's go inside and join our son."

After dinner, we played a short game of Monopoly, and then it was time for bed. I was exhausted from today, but there was nothing more I looked forward to than tucking our son into bed for the night. Shane read him two stories as I listened along.

We all got on our knees and said our prayers. This was for Wyatt, something he did at the group home. He said after all the kids went to sleep, he would climb out of his bed and say his prayers. He would wish for a family to love him. Every night when he gave his thanks to God, I always shed those few tears and said my thankful prayers along with his.

"Okay, little man, I want you to dream of good things, okay?" Shane said.

"I will, daddy."

I watched Shane bend down to place a kiss on his forehead, and then it was my turn to do the same.

"I love you, sweet boy. See you in the morning."

"I love you too, mommy." The sweetest five words I will never tire of hearing.

23

My loves

Shane

There wasn't anything in this world that brought me more happiness than watching my beautiful wife with our son. It had been the best six months of my life. It had been a while since I'd seen her cry, and seeing her in the arms of Jagger today did not sit well with me. It wasn't jealousy, not of Jagger, more like concern for my wife and why she was in such a state. She could never hide her feelings from me. I knew we would talk about it, but for the moment all I wanted to do was lose myself in my wife for a while, and that's exactly what I did.

"Lay back. Close your eyes," I issued my commands as I placed a kiss on her lips.

She did with no hesitation. I loved when she submitted to me with complete trust. She was probably thinking I had something in mind for us tonight, but she would be wrong. I just wanted to simply make love to her. I had this overwhelming feeling of missing her today, and the minute I saw her face, I knew why. It was the connection between us. It was always strong and usually always right.

I undid her blouse to reveal her pale pink lacy bra. Her nipples were already erect through the thin material. I bit down on one as I twisted the other between my two fingers, allowing Shelby to softly cry out in pleasure.

"Shhh, we don't want this to be over before it begins."

Her eyes closed, and I knew she was willing herself not to come. I undid her top button and pulled down her zipper, only to discover she wasn't wearing any underwear.

"Naughty girl, where's the matching bottoms to your bra?" I asked.

"I believe you tore them the last time I wore them, and I haven't had time to replace them."

"Good answer, baby. I kind of like you going bare, but just make sure no one else knows about it. We have a lot of men on this ranch, and no one gets to see what's mine."

"Only yours, Shane."

Once she was completely bare to me, I slid two fingers inside of her very wet and inviting pussy. Her ass bucked up in the air as I hit the right spot to make her scream my name.

"Shhh, quiet, or you don't get to come."

As I worked her over, I knew she was close, and I went in for the kill, causing Shelby to scream into a pillow. I fucking loved getting her all worked up into a heated frenzy. I feasted on her wet folds and lapped up every bit of her sex as I played with her clit and hit her core over and over again.

The evidence of her orgasm was slowly dripping down the insides of her thigh, and before she could utter a word, I was pushing my way inside of her. She grabbed my hips as I pushed deeper and deeper until I filled her. My hands found hers, and I pressed them down to the mattress.

"Open your eyes. Don't look away from me. I love you so much. I love our life, and I promise you that whatever is bothering you, I am going to make you forget. Do you understand me?"

"Yes, I understand," she weakly answered.

"Do you trust me?"

"Yes, with everything I have."

"Okay, then enjoy the ride."

I crushed my mouth on hers and plunged my tongue deep inside. I wanted to mark every inch of her and banish all her fears away once and for all. She cried out her release, and pools of tears flowed from her crystal blue eyes.

I never came so hard and poured my cum inside of her, filling her to her brim until I had nothing left. I was spent and supported by my body above hers as I remained buried inside of my wife. We were both panting and sweat was dripping down my spine as I bent down to lick her chest and make my way down to her taut nipples.

When I finally managed to move, she was already sleeping. It had been a while since we shared a moment like this one tonight. I carefully got out from our bed and got a washcloth from the bathroom. I tried to gently wipe her sex so she wouldn't be uncomfortable when she woke up. She barely moved until the heat from the cloth hit her oversensitive breasts and pussy.

Our lovemaking was always intense, but tonight it needed to be a little rough. It was the only way to bring Shelby back from wherever she allowed her anxiety to lead her. I knew it, and so did she. I climbed back into bed with her and pulled her close to my body, holding her in place.

"Sleep, baby. No more worrying, okay? I love you." I said and soundly fell asleep too.

When the alarm began to sound in the darkness of our bedroom, I hit the stop button and repositioned myself behind Shelby. I wasn't going anywhere today, and once we got Wyatt off to school, I would be having a serious talk with my wife. I placed a kiss on her bare shoulder and left her sleeping while I took a shower.

When I came back out, she was now sitting up in bed with her back against the headboard and the sheet pulled up to her chest, covering everything that I loved.

"Good morning. How are you feeling?" I asked her.

"You really have to ask after that workout last night?"

"No, I kind of know, but I do love hearing how I rate?"

"Oh, cowboy, you more than rate. You literally have the power to make me forget my own name. Thank you for yesterday and last night. I really needed to forget, even if it was for a little while."

"Why is that? What's bothering you, baby? We haven't been here in a long time, and I thought all the ghosts of our past were buried a long time ago."

"Shane, I swear to you I am not going off the rails again. You have to believe I would be upfront and honest with you if I was. I just had an appointment yesterday with Dr. Whitfield. She signed off on concluding our therapy sessions, because she knows I am focused on what is important."

"Okay, tell me this, and please don't lie to me..."

"I promise."

"You need to tell me what is making you so afraid, and then you need to allow me to help you not to be. Look around you, Shelby. We have everything we always wanted, and he's sleeping just a few feet away."

She placed her head in her hands and then wiped away her tears. Hugging her knees, she looked up at me and shrugged her shoulders. "What do you want me to say? I know I screwed up yesterday with Tenley. It's what I do. I just screw up and never learn from the mistakes I make. Losing our son and then the chance to give you any more children should have taught me that, but sadly, here I am making those quick to react mistakes all over again. It's a never-ending repeat button. Why are you still here with me? I am more than you ever wanted to sign on for."

I literally felt as I was holding my breath after hearing her truth. The moment was right there on the edge of me losing consciousness or raging until I blew the roof off. *After all this time, she still feels as if she is not good enough for me. Why would she ever believe I would just stay and listen to that load of garbage? I love her so much, and I've been trying every single day to rise up to the man that is good enough for her, and not the other way around.*

My entire body was trembling with a thousand emotions. I knew if I stepped closer, I would lose control and not only take her body but make her mind submit to me as well. I knew I had the power to calm and bring her back to center. *Hell, I proved that last night. It's what makes us who we are, and what we share in bed brings us to heightened pleasures that make me feel as high as the sky. I love all the experiences I get to share with my wife, but now is not one of those times. I'm angry and will not go to her until I can regain my composure.*

Instead of running and doing the one thing I have accused her of doing in the past, I stayed and did everything humanly possible to calm and move past my anger. Minutes ticked by even though it felt like hours. She remained where she was, and that was in our bed.

"Shelby, you're not the only one that has made mistakes, ones you believed you would never recover from, but you did—we did. For the part I played, my mistakes were epic, and from then to now, I believe I have owned every last one of them. When we agreed to try again and work on our marriage, I believed it when you promised you would always talk to me. For the most part, you have kept your word to me, but now, it feels we are back there again, and baby, it breaks my heart. You have something inside of you that keeps you stuck and unreachable."

She visibly shifted on the bed, and the sheet that was covering her body suddenly was gone. Like the sexy woman she was, she was baring not just her body but her soul as well.

"Shane, I need you." she panted.

Anything I was feeling when I started this haphazard conversation with her ebbed away as I removed my clothing and climbed back on our bed. My hands found her knees, and I slowly parted them even further than they already were. It didn't take long for me to be inside her, with her hands tangling through my hair to bring me closer. She cried out her release as she rode another orgasm I happily gave her.

I wrapped my arms around her small frame and kept her close as our breathing slowly returned to normal. My eyes were closed, and my body felt relaxed almost to the point of falling back to sleep, and then I heard her beautiful soft tone.

"When Wyatt first came to us, I took the leap of faith and believed in the universe. I convinced myself he was a miraculous sign from the heavens above, and I just knew he was meant to be our son. Once that did happen, I found myself in this euphoric state of pure bliss and happiness. Feeling all those wonderful things flow through me, I also became afraid. It was a fear of losing all the good, and then I would be catapulted back to that dark place when I lost everything I loved and cherished most. So, self-preservation kicked in, and I protected everything I held dear and never wanted to let it go. Unexpectedly running into Roberta yesterday shattered all that resolve, and like you said, I was back there and stuck in a place I didn't want to be in."

I moved quickly, causing Shelby to shift off my chest a bit, but she didn't go far because I cupped her face in my hands and made her look at me.

"No, you never have to be there again. This life we have and have fought to have is real, and it's only going to get better, this I promise you. Please have faith in me, and in us. I love you. No one is going to come in-between our family and jeopardize the happiness we have fought to have. You must believe me. Please, Shelby, tell me you do."

She remained quiet, but her eyes softened, and then she leaned in to kiss me back. I knew she was coming back to me, and once I had her where she needed to be, this is where she would remain. I knew she needed positive reinforcement, and I would do whatever it takes to make her feel secure. It took me years of therapy with Wendy to get me here to a place where I felt secure. I knew I made the colossal mistakes of my youth that defined my future years, and then I met Shelby, and she changed my perspective on all things. She made me open my eyes to what was important and fought her way in my heart, and that's where she stayed. Even when I was battling the demons of my past, she was there.

We had gone through more heartache than most couples would ever do in a lifetime. We faced the dark times where we nearly shattered with pain and loss, and then reveled in the good when we decided to try again, and then Wyatt blessed our lives. I kissed her back with all the love I could put behind that kiss. I wanted to show her how much my love had never wavered and would remain strong for Shelby.

"You are the love of my life, and I promise you with all that I have, I will not allow you to fall. Never again. Please trust me to keep those promises to you, and now to Wyatt."

"You won't leave me?" her voice was shaky.

"Never. Not in this lifetime or the next."

Another storm passed, and we survived once again. Because I was up so early, it felt like we'd been talking for hours, but that wasn't the case. The sun was beginning to rise as I made love once more to my wife. We knew we couldn't go back to sleep with Wyatt waking soon. I carried her tired and naked body into the shower and washed her from head to toe, giving her pleasure along the way.

We walked down the wide set of stairs together hand-in-hand and smiling. I made the coffee as Shelby began making the batter for pancakes or waffles, or whatever Wyatt wanted to have this morning. As the coffee brewed, I took my wife in my arms and nuzzled her neck. She giggled, and it was the sweetest sound. We both felt the weight of the world ebb away from the both of us, and then we heard another sweet sound.

"Morning, Daddy! Hi, Mommy! I want pancakes, please."

We both took our turns giving our son his morning hugs, and then we enjoyed breakfast together as a family. It was perfect. I looked around to my wife and son, and without a doubt, I was certain of one thing: Some men in life were lucky to have found one love in their life.

I was blessed to have found two.

24

the visit

Shane

Breakfast was probably my favorite time of the day. Wyatt would come bouncing down the stairs, so excited to go to school, asking me a hundred questions on how I would spend my day. Usually, by this time, I would have worked at least four hours on the ranch before coming home to eat with them. I made this my new routine since we adopted our son. I wanted him to feel as stable as he could under our roof with two parents that loved him to the moon and back.

Yesterday was hard, and last night and this morning were even harder to bear, but Shelby and I moved past all the stress and somehow managed to smile, laugh, and find the simple normalcy of just being together.

I told Shelby to leave the dishes and go back upstairs to sleep. I would take Wyatt to the bus stop, and then I had to take care of a few things in town. She agreed with no argument, and I was thankful for that small win. I didn't want to be the cause of any more stress for her, but I knew where I needed to be, and the one person who could help me above anyone else.

"Well, this is a welcomed surprise. I was just thinking about you the other day and wanted to call you up to get together for dinner, and now you're here," exclaimed a very happy Wendy as she took me in for a hug. "Now, what brings you all the way out here?"

I sighed and then took a seat. I never could hide anything from Wendy.

"Shane, talk to me. What's on your mind?"

"You've always been straight with me, right?"

"Is that a serious question?"

"Please, Wendy, no jokes right now."

"Yes, I have always told you the truth, even the ones that may have hurt you."

"I know. You're also the keeper of secrets, mine included. I need to know something about Tenley, and I have a feeling you know about it."

"Go on."

"I've done my best not to question the things I didn't fully under-stand and trust that everything happens for a reason. In my case, I put my faith and trust in the hands of someone I knew who could and would make the impossible a reality."

"Shane, I'm not following."

"Don't do that, Wendy, not to me. I need to know the truth, and I know you know what that is, as well as Jagger. It's time for me to know."

"Shane, unless you directly say the words, I do not know what you are referring to. As you said, I am the keeper of many secrets."

Okay, here goes nothing. "What did Tenley do to secure our adop-tion of Wyatt? What should have taken at least a year or more, only took less than a month for us to adopt him, and I've been trying in ear-nest to convince my wife that the bottom is not going to fall out from under us and we have nothing to fear, especially when it comes to los-ing our son. Jagger told me to be grateful for the gift I've been given and not to question it. He used Jamie's memory to manipulate me into believing this was some miracle that happened and I was finally a father. I can't lose Wyatt, and if we do, I don't think Shelby would survive it."

"Shane, to use the word 'manipulate' is harsh and unwarranted, especially when used in the same sentence as Jagger and Jamie. His memory is locked and sealed and lives on in all of you. Although we lost Jamie, Jagger is still here. He is your best friend and brother. He would never hurt you, nor would Tenley. You three have such a complicated past that goes longer than most should. They love you, and you love them. There is nothing they wouldn't do for you. The binds of friendship between you three are strong and forever unbreakable. Your fates were sealed a long time ago and I know Shelby has had difficulty understanding what all that means, but it should be as clear as day for you."

"You're not answering my question."

"I don't have to, because you already know the answer. I'm telling you straight. You don't have anything to worry about, and I swear to you on Jamie's memory that is the truth. You need to let this go and help your wife do the same."

"I'm trying. How can I do that? She's so incredibly happy, and then there are times where she is so skittish, she's afraid of her own shadow. I mean, what is it? How can I protect my family if I don't know what I'm protecting them from?"

"Shane, your family is safe, I promise you. You are a good man and an amazing father to that little boy. You have so many people in your life, including me, who love you and will always have your back. You need to remember this and stop allowing your mind to question things that are just not there, okay?"

"I do trust you, Wendy. I always have. I have to go. Thanks for seeing me today."

I hugged my friend and decided to take a drive to clear my head. I felt like a walking contradiction. I say one thing and behave totally different. This is not me to be this uncertain. I know I was kind of reckless in my younger years, but not anymore. I have worked incredibly hard to right the wrongs of my past and to live in the now with my wife. She was there for me every step of the way, and even though we went through our tough times, we came out stronger. *She is strong. I just have to remind her of that, and then we can be strong together.*

Three days later, it was Saturday and the day of Roberta's home visit. Although Shelby wanted Tenley to be here just in case any legal questions come up, I told her no and that we would be fine. Roberta told me on the phone all was well and she just wanted to stop in and say hello to Wyatt.

She did ask me about Rosie and if we changed our mind about telling Wyatt of her passing. He hadn't mentioned her since her first visit to the ranch, and I wasn't going to say or do anything that would make him sad, not when he had made so much progress. He was healthy and happy, and we wanted him to remain that way. I did tell Roberta that if he should ask, then we would decide how to proceed, but it would be our decision on what that might be. She let the subject drop, and she just chatted with our son.

"So, Wyatt, you've told me about school, your friends, and your horse, Joker. How about you tell me about you? How do you like living here at the ranch, and with the Rhodes?"

Shelby gripped my hand as we stood in the doorway listening to their conversation. She was too anxious to sit, so we stayed back and gave Wyatt some time with Roberta. He seemed very comfortable answering her questions, and she seemed pleased with what he said to her.

"I love it here. I have a big bedroom with my own bed and lots of toys. I get to help out down in the barn with Luke and Wade, and I even got to see Bonnie have her baby. It was on a Saturday, so I stayed up all night in the barn until the baby arrived. Right, daddy?"

"That's right, son. We did," I said.

"Wow! You have a pretty good life here on the ranch. How do you feel about the Rhodes? Do they treat you well?"

Wyatt appeared to be uncomfortable with her question and I was about to put a stop to this, but he surprised us both with his answer.

"Ms. Roberta, why do you keep saying, 'The Rhodes?' They're my mommy and daddy, and I love them a lot, and mommy makes the best pancakes ever."

At that moment, Shelby released my hand and walked over to sit by Wyatt, taking him in her arms. He returned her hug and asked if he could go visit Joker. Before answering, she looked at me and then back to Roberta.

"Um, are we done here?" I asked point blank, wanting to end this visit so we could return to our son, our family.

"Yes, we are," she answered and then smiled confidently that she got what she came for. "Wyatt, it was wonderful to spend some time with you."

"Nice to see you too," he said, and then with the green light to go see Joker, he practically bounced off Shelby's lap.

"Go on, son. Luke is outside waiting for you."

"Alright! Thanks, daddy."

I joined Shelby on the couch and then waited for whatever Roberta would say. She jotted down some notes and then pulled out another file and stamped the bottom sheet.

"I want to say thank you for allowing me to come out and spend some time with you. I really couldn't be happier with how your family has evolved. He seems very happy and content with his new life. I hope you understand why I needed confirmation of that."

"We do, and thank you so much for all you have done for our family," Shelby said.

"It's my pleasure. If it wasn't for Tenley bringing this case to my attention, he may have still been in foster care, but I'm happy to say it all worked out. This is for you."

"What is it?" I asked.

"It's a document that I have signed, and when I get back to my office, I will submit my final report, and your file will officially be closed. I have no reason to return here and do another home visit. I am more than satisfied with what I have seen."

We both got up and thanked her again. I kissed my wife and walked Roberta out to her car.

"Roberta, if I may just ask a question."

"Sure, Mr. Rhodes, what is it?"

"It's Shane, please."

"Okay, Shane, what do you want to know?"

"Back there, you mentioned if it wasn't for Tenley bringing our case to you. Would you mind enlightening me on that?"

"I'm sorry if that came out ambiguous. I've known Tenley for a good number of years, and her record speaks for itself. She's a damn good lawyer and fights, let's just say, the injustice of the world, as I do from my little corner of it. Wyatt's case was unique, and I'm very happy it had a happy ending."

"Me too." Listening to my heart and my gut, I accepted her answer and vowed to never question the how and why again.

"You take care of your family, Shane."

"Well? Is everything okay?" Shelby asked as I came back inside. I lifted my wife into my arms and kissed her passionately on her lips.

"Yes, it's more than okay, and it will be tomorrow, and the day after that, and the day after that, and so on. No more doubts, baby, no more. He's ours! He belongs to us, and we belong to him. We are a family, now and forever."

"Yes, forever. Shane, I love you so much. You have made all my dreams come true from our very beginning, and now that our family is complete with Wyatt as our son, I'm so over with my doubts."

"I promise you, baby, you will never know another day of sadness."

"You always keep your promises, this I know without a doubt. You feel like taking a ride with our son?"

"Sounds perfect, lead the way."

We took the horses down by the river. Shelby was by my side, and

Wyatt was settled in front of me while riding on Yankee. He wanted to ride Joker, but he wasn't ready for that just yet. I loved that I could share this with him, just as my dad did with me. When we lost Ryder, we believed our hopes and dreams died along with him, but that didn't happen.

"Daddy, can we skip some stones across the water?"

"Absolutely, I'll show you how grandpa showed me."

"Shane, look how happy he is. This is a dream."

"Yeah, baby, one that has finally come true."

Wyatt wanted to stay for us to watch the sunset, but it was getting cold and we needed to get back. Sunsets were great, but I showed him something better once we got back home.

"Look at all the stars in the sky, daddy. There must be a million up there."

"Millions and millions, but what I really want you to see is that big and shiny one right over there. You see it, son?"

"I see the star, daddy. It looks like it's on top of the mountain."

"It is. He likes it over there."

"Who?"

"Someone special who I will tell you about someday. Anytime you look up to the sky and see that big and shiny star, just know, son, a very special angel is loving you and watching you from way up there."

"Just like you and mommy down here?"

"Yes, exactly like that."

THE END

BONUS SCENE
Tenley's truth

The entire drive back to my house, I was beyond livid with the assumptions Shelby had so boldly made about me. I swear if this was anyone else, I would have gutted them with a spoon. With my gladiator days long behind me, I thought that same persona was too, but maybe it's still there under the veneer of my life here in Wyoming.

I wouldn't say life here is boring; on the contrary, I've taken some interesting cases since my return. Like New York, I still have the power to choose what cases utilizes my talents and what will give me the most satisfaction when I annihilate my opposing counsel in court. Yes, Shelby wasn't wrong when she reminded me of the Bornarelli case, but that was way different from what she demanded of me now.

The syndicate mob family was responsible for literally ruining and ending lives. They preyed on the misfortune of others and made a lot of money in doing so. No, their reign of terror needed to end, and I took much pleasure in bringing them down. What Shelby just asked of me was crossing the line, and I didn't appreciate her brazen attitude.

I immediately felt better once I walked in to my house and my amazing son walked straight into my arms. His small hands reached for my face and pulled me in for a messy, wet kiss.

"Hmmm, Jamie, I smell bananas. Have you been eating bananas?" I asked my boy as he planted another kiss on my cheek, giggling as he did it.

"Mama, I love nanas."

"I know you do, but your fingers are sticky. Where's your daddy?"

He pointed in the direction of the kitchen and then wiggled his way out of my arms. He practically sprinted toward the kitchen, probably warning Jagger that I was home. I braced myself for the disaster I knew would be waiting for me in there, but surprisingly, my pristine kitchen was exactly that. I raised my eyebrow at Jagger and questioned where the pile of dirty dishes was hiding. He laughed and greeted me with a much-needed kiss and then a long hug.

"What's the matter, baby? You look stressed."

"I am. It was quite the afternoon and not what I expected."

"Okay, hold that thought. Let me get Jamie cleaned up and then down for a nap. I'll be right back, and then we can talk."

"Sounds good."

I gave my little boy a kiss and waved him off as Jagger gave him a piggy back ride up the stairs. I knew it was already late for his nap, but if I could get a few minutes with Jagger, I think that would help my mood.

I knew he would be furious if he saw me drinking anything but water, but on the rare occasion, I did indulge in a glass of red wine. For the longest time after our reunion, he detested and forbade all and everything alcohol. He said it reminded him of the time we were apart, and if I could just agree that I wouldn't drink, it would make him very happy. Over the years, he softened, and once in a while, he would have a beer or two with Shane or one of the ranch hands. I never said anything to him, so I hope he gives me the same respect.

I chose no on the wine and poured myself a finger of bourbon. I enjoyed the smooth velvety feel of my choice, Knob Creek. I kicked off my heels and pulled out my blouse that was neatly tucked under my pencil skirt.

I had just come from my office in town with all the files to deliver to Shelby. I never thought I would be ambushed with her demands once I got there. A few minutes later, Jagger came down with the monitor in hand and a disappointed look on his face when he saw the amber liquid in my hand. I was looking off to our mountain view as I swirled around the bourbon in the glass.

"Please, no judgment, not today."

"Must have been pretty bad to reduce you to your hidden stash."

"What?"

"Come on, Tumbleweed, don't play the innocent card here. Yes, I have always known you drink from time to time, but I haven't said anything because it's not excessive and you have given me the same courtesy. I will concede on the one glass you are holding and hope you will not opt for a refill."

"Yes, this is enough. Thank you for understanding."

"Right back at you, babe. Now, tell me what's wrong?"

I sighed and finished off my drink. "As you know, I stopped at Shelby and Shane's house to go over what to expect for Wyatt's upcoming custodial hearing. I was yammering on with Shelby about all the legal do's and don'ts, and then she just stopped me and shocked me with what she said next."

"Which was?"

"She basically accused me of being this shark of a lawyer that could yield her magic and make the standard waiting period go away, and let's say, use my power of persuasion tactics for the greater good and move up the hearing date for not just emergency custody of Wyatt, no, also for the final step that usually takes about a year to eighteen months, if you're lucky."

"And, how did you respond?"

"How do you think? I told her no."

"I'm guessing the conversation didn't end there?"

"You guessed right. She went on to remind me of how I was this big and bad New York City lawyer that bent the rules when I needed something to go in my favor. I adamantly denied that, and then she basically called me a liar and told me that Shane had told her all about how I fucked over the Bornarelli's and successfully took down a major mob family. It wasn't pretty, Jagger. I kept myself in check and fired back, but it fell on deaf ears. She said with our family's money and power, I could definitely sway a court officer or two if I wanted to. There's something else too."

"Don't stop now, babe. You can tell me anything."

"She brought up our past, as in you, Shane, and me. It hurt. It hurt a great deal to go back there again. I swear, I wanted to scratch her eyes out at that moment."

"Wow! That sounds so unlike Shelby to behave that way."

"Jagger, do we know the same person? How she behaved today was exactly the same way she behaved on the very first day we met. She didn't care how she sounded and who heard her. She was hellbent to drive her point home. She successfully did it then, and she did the same thing today."

"Okay, baby, settle down. I know you're upset and have a right to be, but she's our friend and we are going to help her any way we can."

"Jagger, what are you saying?"

"I love you, that's what I'm saying. Shane's here. Let me go outside and talk to him for a minute. You okay?"

"Yes, I'm fine."

I watched Jagger talk to Shane, as I poured myself another shot of liquid courage. I already knew how I would proceed with Shelby's request, and swallowing the warm liquid eased my mind enough to make the call. I quickly picked up my cell phone and dialed the number before I changed my mind.

"Raymond, hi, yes, it's me. I know it's been a while, but just in case you forgot, motherhood is a full-time job. Yes, he's wonderful. I know, I miss Zoey too. I'll be seeing her over the summer. Yes, I love your plan, but it's not why I called. I need a favor, and it's a pretty big one."

After I concluded my phone call with Raymond Steele, my former boss and mentor from New York, our son woke up, and I focused all my attention on my family. I would handle Shane's tomorrow.

I was holding Jamie in my arms as I called out to Jagger from our porch. Shane waved to me, and he looked like he might have wanted to talk to me, but I wasn't ready for that and I called Jagger inside. The two friends said their goodbyes, and then Jagger quickly ran up to me and took Jamie into his arms and waved off Shane. I waved back and leaned against my front door looking at Jagger. He knew what I had done just by the way he was looking back at me. He gave me the "everything is going to be okay look" and then took me into a hug.

Yes, I knew he was right, because I am a damn good lawyer. I will make this happen for Shane, and then finally a long overdue debt will finally be paid.

"Thank you, your honor, for seeing me today," I said to Judge Clayton.

"Well, to be honest, your call intrigued me, and Raymond Steele assured me that it would be worth my while."

"Yes, that's one way of looking at it."

"So, I can't say I wasn't impressed after reading your file. You had quite the run of successful cases back in New York. What made you leave it all behind?"

"Who says I have?"

"I stand corrected. I wasn't sure if the gladiator was still in there."

"She's never too far away, so let me get to the reason why I'm here."

"Go on."

"Here," I said and handed him a file. "Before I say any more, why don't you have a look?"

He let out an exasperated sigh and began reading the file. His eyebrows rose as he continued to read on. He closed the file and looked back at me, slamming down to the desk.

"Where did you get this?"

"How I obtained that information is not important. What you should be asking is what I intend to do with it?"

"And what might that be?"

"A few weeks ago, a little boy went missing from Cathedral Home for Children and was missing from that facility for over two weeks."

"And? What does that have to do with me?"

"It has everything to do with you. You see, your honor, his disappearance was handled through your jurisdiction. Why wasn't an Amber alert issued? Not even one headline in a local or statewide newspaper. Can you explain that?"

"I'm guessing you already know."

"Yes, I do, and with the knowledge I now have, I am prepared to bury you, and I won't lose a night of sleep over it."

"Tenley..." he warned.

"You may call me Ms. Fairchild."

"What will it take for this to go away?"

"Corruption never really goes away, now, does it, your honor? Let's just say I have begun to pave the way to clean house, and I will begin with Cathedral. The children that reside in that group home will be assigned to loving families by the end of the week, or you and your wife will be brought up on a multitude of charges that I will personally bring to the State Attorney's office."

"Ms. Fairchild, please, you don't understand."

"Enlighten me, I have the time. I appreciate your problem, and your intentions may have been sincere when it comes to protecting your wife and her grave errors in judgment, but her duplicity also put every child under her charge in danger, especially Wyatt Jacoby."

"I can assure you I have taken the necessary steps to handle my wife."

"That may be, but it's not enough, not by a long shot. I still intend to pursue everything I have already disclosed to you."

"And? If that's true, then why come to me at all?"

"Because I need a favor, one that will benefit the two of us."

"So, this entire speech of you being the big crusader of the greater good, you're really here to blackmail me?"

"Oh, I still intend to kick ass for the greater good, and blackmail is such a dirty word. Let's call this a negotiation."

"Fine! What do you want?"

"I want Wyatt Adam Jacoby placed in permanent custody. I have a family willing to adopt him."

"Okay, that can be arranged. I will sign off on the paperwork and get everything started for you."

"No, you misunderstand. Let's skip all the laps and cross the finish line with a hearing and a granted petition for adoption. This boy has been through hell and has to endure more disappointment and heart-ache than anyone should have to. I have two people who were meant to be parents who already love him and will give this child an amazing life. I need a signature and a time-slot on your Monday morning calen-dar."

"And? What do I get in return?"

"For one, you, your honor, get to still remain on the bench with your wife kept out of jail. I can take down the house without burying her along with it. It's your choice. There is no time left on this offer. What's it going to be?"

"Done. I'll see you Monday morning at 9:00. Does that work for you?"

"It does. Thank you for seeing things my way." I grabbed my things and opened the door to his chambers.

"Oh, Ms. Fairchild, one question, please?"

"Yes, *your honor?*" I enunciated those words very slowly, because once upon a time, he actually had that.

"Did I really have a choice to not grant your request?"

"You read my file. What do you think?"

I chose to return to my office in town instead of going back home to the ranch. I needed some time to allow the adrenaline to subside and clear my head. I never wanted a drink so much in my life, but I knew I wasn't going to do that.

As I predicted, Raymond phoned me shortly after my visit with Judge Clayton. "So, you really did it. You used the file against Clayton."

"Did you believe I would just sit on something that explosive?"

"I taught you better."

"Yes, you did, but you also taught me that sometimes as much as the law works, there are loopholes in it and people get hurt sometimes. I had the opportunity to save someone today, and I absolutely would do it again and again."

"Somehow, that's what I thought you would say. You know, he's not a bad man. He just made some bad decisions."

"Well, today he made a good one. Thank you, Raymond. I won't forget this."

"You know I would do anything for you."

"I do know that. I love you too. Listen, someone just walked into my office, I'll talk to you soon."

I hung up my phone, and it felt like déjà vu all over again, but this time I wasn't in New York.

"Hi, Wendy."

"Hi, yourself, Tumbleweed. By the looks of you, I'm guessing rough day?"

"It wasn't too bad when you consider it will have a happy ending?"

"For you?"

"No, for Shane."

"Are you okay?"

"No, but I will be."

"Come on, Tumbleweed, I thought you let that go a long time ago. It's ancient history."

"Wendy, it may have seemed that way but it wasn't, and I was recently reminded of that fact. When I came back home after the years I was away, all I could do was focus on Jagger recovering from his accident, and as you know, I was still carrying around a lot of emotional baggage. You should know, Wendy. You had a front seat to all the carnage I left behind. I hurt Jagger, and then my foolish mistake hurt their friendship, and they both hated me in the end."

"That's not true, and you know it. This is not a trip down memory lane that I want you to take. That time in your life is in the past, and that's where it will remain. If what you did today was your penance for something that you did back in college, then you have more than made up for it after what you did for Shane and Shelby today. Come here, sweetheart." Wendy had her arms open wide for me to walk right into for one of her best hugs.

"Wendy, I guess it goes without saying that this conversation is between us, right?"

"Keeper of secrets, right?"

"That you are. I love you, Wendy."

"I love you more, Tumbleweed. Now, you have your cowboy and your mini cowboy in training waiting for you."

I drove home with a lighter heart. As always, Wendy was right. The past is the past. We have so much to be grateful for. I smiled knowing how true that was, and now today, Shane has everything he always wanted.

Yeah, I can live with that.

A NOTE FROM THE AUTHOR

Thank you, readers, for taking the time to read *Shane*. I hope you enjoyed my cowboy as much as I loved writing his story. Although this novel is standalone, the characters originated from the novel *All Roads Lead Home*. I received many messages asking me to write more for Shane but at the time, I felt his story was complete with getting his happily ever after with Shelby. It took me some time to reach a decision, and once I began to outline his story, I knew I couldn't stop at that point. These characters are very special to me, especially Jamie. I know I put them through a lot but in the end, I hope I delivered the ending you wanted.

Please go to the retailer where you purchased this book and write a review. Even if it's just a line or two, it's the best gift you can give back to an author. They are always welcomed and appreciated.

Thank you for supporting my work.

Mary

ACKNOWLEDGMENTS

Thank you, God, for giving me the ability to create my art.
Thank you, to my family who love me unconditionally.
Thank you, to my friends who never let me fall.

Thank you,
to the talented professionals that make my work come to life.

Thank you, Joe Marron. My editor.
You get me, and I love you for that.
Thank you, Julie Titus, @ JT Formatting.
Your creativity knows no bounds.
Thank you, Francessca, @ Francessca's PR & Design.
You are a cover goddess.

And…

Thank you, to my readers. You mean so much to me. I truly appreciate
you reading and supporting my work. Thank you, to my blogger
friends. You work incredibly hard for authors in this community.

SHANE

Thank you, for always sharing the love. Writing has become an essential part of my soul, and without it, I would be lost. I am forever thankful for the gift I have been given. Thank you, for sharing this incredible journey with me.

OTHER BOOKS BY MARY A. WASOWSKI

Forever Series
Forever: Book One
Second Chance at Forever: Book Two
Our Forever Promise: Book Three
Happily Forever After: Book Four
Forever More: Book Five

Standalone novels
A Changed Life
All Roads Lead Home
An Unfinished Life
Return to Kildare
Revive
You Belong to Me
Run
Broken Dove

ABOUT THE AUTHOR

Mary A. Wasowski is a best-selling author who writes adult contemporary romance. Best known for her *Forever* Series, Mary loves creating sexy alpha book boyfriends for you to swoon over. When she is not writing her happily ever after love stories, she is an avid reader of all romance.

A romantic at heart, she shares her zest for life with her husband, Henry, and their three sons. Proud to be an indie author, she lives in North Carolina and works as a full-time writer.

Stay in Touch!
I would love to hear from you.
Please stay connected wherever you are.

EMAIL:
AuthorMaryAWasowski@gmail.com

FACEBOOK:
https://www.facebook.com/Author-Mary-A-Wasowski-332971356804341

MARY A. WASOWSKI

TWITTER:
https://twitter.com/wasow6

INSTAGRAM:
https://instagram.com/authormaryawasowski/